Never Again So Close

Never Again So Close

CLAUDIA SERRANO

Translated by Anne Milano Appel

amazon crossing

This is a work of fiction. Names, characters, organizations, places, events, and incidents are either products of the author's imagination or are used fictitiously.

Text copyright © 2015 by Claudia Serrano and Giunti Editore
Translation copyright © 2017 by Anne Milano Appel
All rights reserved.

No part of this book may be reproduced, or stored in a retrieval system, or transmitted in any form or by any means, electronic, mechanical, photocopying, recording, or otherwise, without express written permission of the publisher.

Previously published as *Mai più così vicina* in Italy by Giunti Editore. Translated from Italian by Anne Milano Appel. First published in English by AmazonCrossing in 2016.

"Two Letters" from *Opus Posthumous: Poems, Plays, Prose* by Wallace Stevens. Copyright © 1989 by Holly Stevens. Copyright © 1957 by Elsie Stevens and Holly Stevens. Copyright renewed 1985 by Holly Stevens. Used by permission of Alfred A. Knopf, an imprint of the Knopf Doubleday Publishing Group, a division of Penguin Random House LLC. All rights reserved.

"Il signore di fronte" in *Poesie* by Vivian Lamarque. Copyright © 2002, Arnoldo Mondadori Editore S.p.A., Milano. Copyright © 2015, Mondadori Libri S.p.A., Milano.

Excerpt from *Journey to the End of the Night* by Louis-Ferdinand Céline. Copyright © 1934, 1952 by Louis-Ferdinand Céline. Translation copyright © 1983 Ralph Manheim. Reprinted by permission of New Directions Publishing Corp.

Excerpts from *A Writer's Diary* by Virginia Woolf. Copyright © 1954 by Leonard Woolf. Copyright renewed 1982 by Quentin Bell and Angelica Garnett. Reprinted by permission of Houghton Mifflin Harcourt Publishing Company. All rights reserved.

Published by AmazonCrossing, Seattle

www.apub.com

Amazon, the Amazon logo, and AmazonCrossing are trademarks of Amazon.com, Inc., or its affiliates.

ISBN-13: 9781503941489
ISBN-10: 1503941485

Cover design by David Drummond

Printed in the United States of America

*To Professor Mario Ziccolella, my grandfather,
Sunday of my eyes*

Write like you can forget,

write and forget.

Hold an entire world in your palm

then puff.

Pierluigi Cappello

1

Thirty-nine. That's the number of moles I counted on his back, thirty-nine.

I've spent many sleepless nights lying beside him. He'd crash after lovemaking, often there wasn't even time to cuddle. I wasn't able to sleep.

Thirty-nine. He would roll over on his side, his back to me. A pale back. I'd start counting. Skin blemishes were not part of the tally, and at times, in the dark, it was hard to make them out, so I would have to start over.

Thirty-nine.

I didn't dare touch him. I traced the outline of his forms, my finger in the air, less than an inch from his skin. The curve of his pelvis, the slight slope of his back, the sharpness of the shoulder blades.

If, by mistake, my finger lingered over an area, if the desire to stroke it violated the space between my flesh and his, I would draw back quickly.

You can caress a man even from a distance. You can reach him, and let yourself be reached, even without touching him. You can lose everything the moment you give in to the temptation to do so.

You can reject the word "love" and disguise it with a number: thirty-nine. And all that is what he taught me.

My name is Antonia. Names are important: when you name things, they exist.

My professor of French literature would often say that, when we sat lost for hours, our heads deep in nineteenth-century novels. "Note the importance of language in matters of the heart," he would say as the last of the afternoon light filtered through the transom windows. "When Adolphe writes to Ellénore, he pours all his uncertainties into his letter; yet his own words of love make him begin to feel the things he writes. That is the foremost fundamental law: language has the power to create reality. When spoken, a thing exists."

Some years later, one sunny day on the Aventine Hill, it would be Vittorio's turn to add a tile to the mosaic when he spoke about DeLillo's book and naming the parts that make up a shoe: "So the Jesuit priest asks the boy to look at his shoes and name their parts, and he begins to stammer, 'laces, sole, heel,' but that's as far as he can go. At which point the Jesuit tells him that he doesn't see the others, the tongue, the eyelets, the counter, because he doesn't know their names. That's the way it is: things remain hidden until we know what to call them."

It was during the time when, dazzled by his presence, I thought it would be the beginning of something that concerned us.

Afterward, well afterward, I was left with just my name, Antonia, having to repeat it to be sure I existed.

Then, somehow, while the others kept coming up with recovery plans—"Better not to ask her anything," "Let's suggest a trip"—and trying to interpret my changes—"She seems less upset," "She's over it"—I discovered that I had been told only part of the story; if it's true that things become real when you call them by name, the opposite is just as true: there are things that persist in existing even when you still can't name them.

And so, the first morning after I returned home from Milan, when I walked into the kitchen and found the table set for breakfast—orange juice and biscotti beside a turned-over cup—the unmentionable thing, the "thing" as Vittorio referred to it if he had to talk about us, was there.

I remember my discomfort at finding those objects laid out to await me, and the voices of my parents whispering in the other room, "She's up."

They came into the kitchen together, sat down in front of me. I had poured the tea, bitten into a biscotto.

"Were these the ones you used to like?"

"Yes, thanks."

"Papa remembered the kind with cream, I told him these were the ones!"

"Yes, these are the ones, but the other kind would have been okay too."

"See the cup I picked for you?"

"Yes, it's pretty."

"And the tablecloth?"

I smiled, brought the cup to my lips, but my hands were shaking. Behind them, outside the window, I saw a clear sky and an expanse of rooftops with TV antennas.

My mother turned to follow my gaze. "You missed these colors in Milan, right?" And I begged God to open a chasm under my chair and let me be swallowed up on the spot, me and the entire tea service and the embroidered tablecloth and the biscotti and the expectant eyes of my mother.

Probably, simply, you have to become acquainted with certain truths: accept the fact that wounds, some wounds, do not heal; that things, some things, don't work out, and that not everyone is spared.

I spent the first few weeks after my return home reviewing lessons I had unlearned. The bedroom floor has a diamond pattern, marbled; I've always hated it. The living room floor is white, the one in the kitchen is pinkish, terra-cotta. The bathroom floor is orange, so kitsch that guests make up excuses to use the toilet. Some nights, the *tramontana* from the north will come and shake up the plants on the terrace, I'll hear the pots skitter from side to side, and Papa will get up to check them, tie things up, swear. The terrace's bricks are scorching hot under your feet on summer evenings. I relearned these things before surrendering to the fact that what had been a part of me no longer pertained to me.

There was nothing left to do but throw on my sweats—me, the girl who used to wear heels just to go to the store—and drive to the seashore to watch the people walk by, following them, at times, because their bodies gave me comfort. The skin of the fat man sprawled out on the beach, for example—I can still remember it, along with the reassuring thought of being able to touch it. If I had done so, my finger would have sunk into the yielding white flesh, between the bluish spiderweb of veins. It cheered me up.

Going back home, I took the wrong street, but I was ashamed to ask for directions in my own city. "I've been away," I would have excused myself.

I used to be with a man who sang a song that said love can bring you to your knees. I slid the disc into the car's CD player, and the first notes were enough to make me crumble. Now I knew what that man meant when he made love with me and whispered, "Can you imagine?"

"What?"

"How beautiful you are. And that we're going to die."

The cars behind me honked their horns.

Sooner or later I managed to find it, the way home. Where do the pieces of us end up, the ones that we traded for a little love?

"If you give, you give," the street that unrolled before my used Twingo said. "It's a simple reckoning, reasonable, acceptable."

Acceptable?

Anyway, my name is Antonia. And that is as true as the color of these tiles and all these real things to which we must now cling.

His name was Vittorio. A substantial name, solid. Sometimes, at night, I look for it in the telephone listing and read it over and over again, his name in capital letters. Then I tap a key and return to the main menu and to my childhood bed; a single bed will be enough to accommodate my paltry future life.

But now I'm becoming melodramatic. After all, I can manage not to be: I can spend hours staring at the pot of azaleas on the windowsill and the cord from the roll-up shutter that just hangs beside the window, doing nothing more than that, all day.

I must have learned to contain myself. Even when I would like to rip out the railings of the terrace and scream, "Let me out of here," I don't. I make a cup of tea, I turn the cup in my hands, I concentrate on the quality of the ceramic. Even if I then find myself reading in the tea those absurd telegraphic e-mails that Vittorio used to send me.

> From: vittorioso@gmail.com
> To: antonia@libero.it
> Subject: Bougainvilleas in Tarutao
>
> White beaches, unspoiled nature, friendly indigenous people. Undrinkable coffee. Nevertheless, the resort offers every comfort for a quality stay. Visual confirmation follows.

When I come back, though, let's go have a pizza. Tell Dukan too (and wear the black sheath).

V.

And I start laughing and then, as I laugh, the tears come.
"Dear Vittorio," I would write him today, "I remember many happy times."

2

The motorcycle skidded around the hairpin turns of the Ligurian coast. Along the roadside, wildflowers exploded. You could smell their fragrance. My head snuggled against Vittorio's back, I saw them quiver as we passed, waves of yellow and orange nodding over the black asphalt. My silk pants billowed and flapped in the wind as the bike sped along; they too had flowers on them.

Ancient villas overlooking the gulf, perched on rocky cliffs, could be glimpsed behind the maritime pines.

"I'd love to be in all those houses," I said. "I'd like to go into every living room, every kitchen, look out from every window. I'd like to see this gulf from that balcony and from that one, and from that other one too!"

Vittorio laughed under the helmet.

"And then . . . then I'd like to open all the credenzas that you can see from the road, touch all the china and coffee services and drink a cup of tea in every house! Don't you think that life in those houses must be beautiful? What can they be doing? Are they about to play tennis? Are they having breakfast on the terrace? I picture them walking barefoot on ultramarine tiles . . ."

"Ultramarine, no less!" he teased. "It seems beautiful to you because it's not your life."

I placed my hands on his hips, I could feel their suppleness under the T-shirt.

"Vittorio, do you think it will always be like that for me? Will I always be on a road, fantasizing about other people's houses?"

What had Vittorio answered? I don't remember. Maybe he hadn't said anything, and I must have bitten my lip and gone back to looking at the sky, which seemed to race along, azure blue, with us.

I heard the key turn in the lock, the memories scurried away to hide in a corner.

Anna found me sitting on the couch, cross-legged, used tissues everywhere. It was seven a.m.

"Already up?" she asked.

"Sort of."

"Maybe you still have to adjust to the new rhythms." She pretended not to notice my red eyes.

Anna doesn't pander to my grief by indulging in little pity parties, doesn't look for a way to console me; she cleans the fish while I have breakfast, boils the turnips as I dunk biscotti in my tea. For her, everything amounts to "That's life," but she has a way of saying it, smiling, not sad, as she shrugs her shoulders.

She's fifty years old and has seven grandchildren. Soon the oldest one will make her a great-grandmother. She says I am lucky to have studied and that there's time for everything else, even though occasionally she asks me when I'm going to find a husband. "You'd better do it before you're thirty," she advises.

"I brought you something," she said, rummaging through the shopping bags.

"For me?"

"Here it is, a Padre Pio cake."

"What?"

"A chain."

She pulled out a plastic cup capped with aluminum foil. I shuffled over to her in my pajamas.

"My sister-in-law gave it to me, and now I'm giving it to you. The starter is in this cup, you just have to follow the recipe. Here's the paper with the instructions, can you read my writing? It takes ten days to make it, every day you have to add an ingredient."

I looked at her, puzzled.

"There are rules, though. You have to start on a Sunday, and you have to leave everything out of the refrigerator, at all times. At the end, you take three cupfuls from the mixture and give them to three people, to continue the chain."

"No, wait, how can it stay out of the fridge for ten days?"

"I don't know, but it turns out good."

I glanced at the sheet with the recipe.

"Ten days to make a cake?"

"Finally, when you put it in the oven, you can make a wish. That's why it takes time, what do you think?"

She went out to the terrace, she always starts cleaning from there.

My father came into the kitchen, eating a yogurt. With his spoon, he pointed to the cup I was holding. "What's that?"

"Nothing."

I stuck the cup in the freezer.

Tonight I attended a birthday celebration.

We were in a restaurant, a kind of girls' night out. Betta asked me about him while we were at the table.

"And Vittorio, do you still think about him?"

I felt the other women's tension, I sensed their legs jerk, stiffening under the table.

Betta is the only one who has the nerve to name him, Vittorio that is; the others think it's better for me if they pretend he never existed. I lowered my eyes, twirled the fork in my plate; the spaghetti obeyed, winding around the tines, and I was just about to come out with it. But it was obscene, the truth. So I waved a hand, driving off the ghost.

"What were we saying?"

The others were quick to change the subject, talking over one another in their eagerness. I thought, Soon enough Betta won't ask me about him anymore either, and then who will name him?

At that point, the cake with a single flickering candle arrived, and we sang "Happy Birthday" to Betta as people watched us from the other tables. Betta blew, we clapped. The whole time, I waited for the moment when, standing in front of the bathroom mirror, I would wipe off my makeup, leaving the dark eyeshadow on the cotton ball.

When I got home, I took the cup out of the freezer, peeled off the foil covering, and peeked inside: it was a disgusting, beige mixture. I sniffed: it stank.

"You can't refuse the cup you're given." I seemed to hear Anna's voice.

"Why not?"

"Because it's something you must care for."

I tried opening a book. I started reading with one of those little clip-on lamps that cling to the page, but the slightest touch was enough to jiggle it so that the light seemed to wobble. I sat in the dark kitchen for a long time, listening to my father snoring a few rooms away, my mother nudging him every now and then: "Mino!"

Vittorio's song played on in my mind, promising to take me away.

And so, I let the mixture in the cup thaw. Then I took a notebook and a pen and started writing these pages.

Why? Maybe because nothing is safe, not even a cup of starter in the freezer.

3

Milan—"M," as I used to call it—a story that cannot be fully told, a knot that has not been untangled.

It was February, and it was snowing inside the station on the day I arrived. The canopy extending over the tracks was damaged, and small flakes sifted down on people and their bags.

The rented apartment was on the fourth floor.

In the evening, I tried tuning in to the TV channels, my supper on the arm of the couch. I would quickly give up and switch it off. I arranged the books on the shelves, hung a painting. I waited for someone who would wipe his shoes on the mat behind the door, notice the wooden ladder with the cacti arrayed on its steps, reach out to the CDs.

I imagined conversations and evenings with new friends sitting around my table: purses piled on the chair, someone smoking at the window. I would fall asleep on the couch, and the next morning, I would buy a set of gelato dishes, new glasses, a corkscrew.

Night, in Milan, descended almost as if invoked. If only to put an end to that gray, if only to have a sky like everyone else's.

"What do you mean, the same as everyone else's? Can't you see that it's orange?" Gioia said to me one day.

"And not one single star. In fact, if you see one, it means it's going to snow the next day!"

Nevertheless, happy hour always came.

A half hour of hustle and bustle leaving the offices, the gates of the Indro Montanelli Gardens closing, bicycle racks emptying. "Where are you? Cadorna? I'm entering the subway, on my way!"

Heels, lipstick, a tram, the Navigli!

"Start getting a table. Ten minutes and we're there!"

On go the hat and gloves, gloves especially if you have to ride a motorbike.

Traffic was gridlocked. The bars were filling up.

"Two white wines, not sparkling. Thank you," could be read on people's lips behind the windows of a bar.

Groups of young women waited in front of a club; then the door opened and they filed in one after the other, their stylish coats disappearing along with hair fragrant from the day's shampoo.

The last undecided ones wavered between one bar and another.

Then, abruptly, total silence. Deserted streets. Only the night sky remained—yes, orange. I returned home and lowered the shutters.

Milan. I learned expressions like "happenings" and "*apericena*," aperitif plus supper buffet. I learned to have nice clothes, but never as nice as those of others. I learned to walk with a straight back, making my boots click-clack loudly. To smile as if I were happier than I was. Because that's how Milan teaches you to become an adult, by pulling the chair out from under you when you're tempted to sag.

But I still kept an eye out for guys reading the sports pages, I still yearned, above all else, for a picnic basket.

Then I met Vittorio.

That day, in the conference room, a bright light shone from the windows. The hostesses placed bottles of water on the speakers' table and tapped the microphones with their fingertips; meanwhile the room was filling up—coats, perfumes, handshakes—while occasional groups of smokers left—just enough time for one last cigarette.

I was already in my seat, having arrived half an hour early, my coat, carelessly folded on the chair, pressing behind my back. I was waiting for Laura, the only person I knew in Milan, who had invited me to that publishing conference and now hadn't shown up.

It was a luminous, aimless Saturday.

Some water had pooled in a saucer under a flowerpot on the windowsill. Passing clouds covered and exposed the sun so that its rays struck the stagnant transparency of the water and then retreated, casting yellow reflections and recapturing them, making the bits of soil on the bottom gleam.

Everything hovered on the thin edge of anticipation, and that light told me that once the conference ended, I would do something foolish, I would go to Via della Spiga and buy some new panty hose, special panty hose.

A shoe invaded the square of light that the window traced on the floor. A dark brown loafer.

The gaze of the man wearing the shoe fell on my legs. I too looked at them: bony knees in flesh-colored hose. In Milan, everyone knows you don't wear flesh-colored hose. Awkwardly, I tugged my skirt down to cover my knees. When I looked up, the man was gone.

"Oh thank goodness you're here! I'm late, I know!"

Laura, a stout-bodied woman, made her way through the crowd, wiping sweat from her forehead with a tissue. "Excuse me, may I . . ." A blissful smile spread over her face when I stood up to greet her; she raised her arms as though reciting the Lord's Prayer and screamed, "*Bellaaa!*" She hugged me forcefully. Then she sank into her chair, and the whole row felt the repercussion.

She fished a chocolate out of her pocket—did I want one?—popped it in her mouth, closed her eyes.

"Scrumptious!"

I smiled.

"Look how sunny it is," she went on as she struggled with her coat, trying to take it off. "And to think of what the forecast was!"

"Milan always does what it wants," I replied, helping her free her arm from a sleeve.

"And in Venice there's a flood alert, the taxi driver told me. We're almost at high tide, but unscathed!" She laughed loudly.

The first annoyed shhhes spread through the room, a few more moments of bustling around—"A journalist with no pen, do you have one I can borrow?"—then silence.

Vittorio was one of the first publishers to speak. I followed him as he made his way from the first row to the microphone on the speakers' podium. He was young, not very tall. He walked the few feet with a faint spring in his step, as if wanting to get a running start. He was the man with the loafers in the square of light.

"Vittorio Solmani, a good reason to come and endure these conferences!" Laura sighed.

"What do you mean?"

The women sitting in front of us elbowed one another. Laura put a hand over her mouth to hide her laughter.

The first thing I thought, however, when I saw that guy get up to speak, was that he would do well to trim those seventies sideburns and ditch the tweed plaid jacket he was wearing.

"I find him so fascinating," Laura murmured.

Was that all you had to do to be appealing in Milan, pretend you rummaged through a vintage flea market?

Vittorio entered my life that day, accompanied by a comment on his allure, and I don't think I've ever forgiven him for it.

"'The miles of distance away / from everything would end. It would all meet.'" He began his talk with that quote. Without clearing his throat. Which was striking, inviting, somber.

"On my way here this morning . . . ," he improvised.

His hair was salt-and-pepper, artfully disheveled; he had horn-rimmed glasses, as dictated by hipster fashion of the moment. And he wore an earring, as if to say, "I have a position, but I'm not a conformist."

The men in the audience were slumped in their seats, legs crossed, arms condescendingly folded over their chests. Laura was taking notes, accompanying every word by nodding her head of thick, curly hair.

What was his trick?

His face revealed few expressions; from time to time he smiled briefly, the only movement on his tanned face. Still, those smiles lit it up, and this was probably not planned. Or maybe it was, because at regular intervals he would imperceptibly lean toward the audience, and the middle-aged women with Botoxed lips clung to their seats.

He talked about a recent trip in a Ford Fiesta. "We'd meet at the bar in the *piazza*, Giovanni and Gabriele and I, and hold impromptu discussions inspired by Malvasia." He gave us time to marvel over the fact that he did not have an Audi.

"Giovanni Ascolti and Gabriele Galli, the founders of the publishing house Marea," Laura whispered in my ear.

"Oh."

Silence floated through the room when he closed his mouth. The seconds hung suspended between us and him, in midair, as if surprised to be there. But then Vittorio took off his glasses, smiled, said, "Thank you," and time obeyed that smile and began to flow again. The audience applauded, and the seconds too returned to their place, in the ticking of the clocks.

Well done, Solmani, but I'll figure out what your trick is.

He shook his curly, graying head of hair, a laughing, ironic gesture (was he responding to my threat?), and meanwhile the sun had shifted and the square of light on the floor had lengthened to reach my legs.

During the coffee break, Laura introduced me to her friends. I shook hands, I repeated my name several times and instantly forgot those of the others. Then they all went back to listening to her, leaving me at the edge of the circle they had formed around her.

I held my clutch bag under my arm and felt silly not to have left it in the room as the others had.

I made my way to the beverage table though I wasn't thirsty.

A girl shouted Vittorio's name from across the room. I turned and saw her dash into his arms.

"It's been so long!"

He greeted her with polite detachment, laughing, I thought, at her effusion. They approached the table. "So, tell me what you've been up to," Vittorio began. He waved the waiter off, no problem, he himself poured some juice for the girl, who had a nose ring and dark bangs falling over her eyes (she must have been more or less my age, I estimated, and she was rather ugly), and clinked their glasses in an intimate toast. Out of place, I thought. I looked away and slipped off as soon as possible.

I ran into Vittorio again in the conference room, before the others came back, as he was putting his notes in a satchel. I passed him as I returned to my seat, so close that I could read the title of a book he was putting back in his briefcase. Recognizing it, I said to him, "I read it and I loved it."

He looked up. Behind the oversized glasses, a pair of unsettling blue eyes. I quickly turned away and recovered my composure by spotting an abandoned fur on a chair.

"I'm really glad. He's one of our best authors, unfortunately still largely unknown in Italy."

I thought I saw amazement in his eyes, a kind of childlike surprise. He was still bent over the open briefcase, paused in the act of putting the volume away.

"Have you read other books in our catalog?"

"*Desires.*"

"Damn, the worst seller of all time!" He laughed.

I shrugged.

He straightened up, leaving the briefcase open, the book still in his hand. Where was the seductive publisher who had spoken from the speakers' podium? Standing before me was just a guy, and we were the same height.

Did I know that the author often came to Italy? he asked me. He had a house in Sicily.

I wondered why I had stopped to talk to him. That guy was simply sorting things out: one minute time stops, the next it resumes its course, then this girl who doesn't know how to apply makeup and has splotches of foundation on her face comes up and talks to him.

Actually, Vittorio was talking and smiling. When he added something about happiness, I backed away from his cheerfulness because it seemed like something to defend against.

Soon the other attendees began returning to the room. Now voices had to be raised to be heard; mine was so low that Vittorio had to keep leaning toward me to have me repeat my words in his ear. So I let him go on talking, and I merely nodded.

"May I get by?" someone behind me asked. Before I could move, Vittorio pulled me toward him, and I found myself a few inches from his tweed jacket. He took his hand off my shoulder. "He was in Brooklyn." He picked up the thread of the conversation without batting an eye; I, however, stepped back and crossed my arms over my chest, and in so doing, lost my grip on the clutch bag.

"Well," I said, hurriedly picking it up from the floor, "I'm going back to my seat."

"We'll say good-bye, then?" Vittorio shielded his eyes from a ray of sun coming through the window, a tiny gesture that stuck in my memory. "A gorgeous day today." He winked, holding out his hand.

"It's sunny in Venice as well, but the water is rising over an inch every half hour," I explained, on the defensive.

Vittorio looked at me quizzically, then smiled placidly. "I'll stay in town, then," he said.

And I, already in over my head, returned to my seat.

"They invited us to the restaurant, at the end of the conference," Laura whispered.

"I'd rather go home, thanks. Are you going?"

"Of course, after such a day! And besides all these boring old dodderers, Solmani will be there. Sure you don't want to come?"

"Still going on about this Vittorio?"

"How on earth can you not like him?"

Looking around for him, I found his salt-and-pepper curls, his purposely unkempt beard, the marmoreal profile.

"He's not my type," I replied, shaking my head.

4

Day One: Pour the mixture into a glass bowl. Add a cup of flour and a cup of sugar. DO NOT MIX.

If Vittorio only knew.

"Padre Pio cake?" His eyes would widen.

"Yeah, okay, that's what it's called, maybe because there's a final wish that will come true, or rather, that should come true, though no one really believes that . . ."

"I didn't think such things still existed in the twenty-first century!" He would shake the ash off the cigarette, a wry smile on his lips.

"A southern legacy," I would reply, then, annoyed, "like the trousseau and all the rest!"

"Don't tell me you have a trousseau . . . Do you have a trousseau?"

But on the tenth day, I know, he'll surprise me with a text message: *Weren't you going to finish the cake today?*

Vittorio.

Anyway, I followed the recipe.

I took the cup with the revolting starter, and I emptied it into a glass bowl. I used the same cup to add the flour and sugar, and I did not mix them. I stood there, staring at the sugar and flour piled atop the initial mass.

What's the point of throwing things on top of one another and leaving them separate? But maybe that's the first mistake: the rush to mix together, to make two into one. The eagerness to lose oneself in the other.

Vittorio would never make such a mistake.

"What do you need to do this morning?" My mother came into the kitchen. "Come with us?" She took some steaks out of the freezer.

"I can't."

"Do you have an article you have to hand in?"

"Yes."

Instead, I picked up the pen to write these silly lines, to say that it was Sunday and while the others went for a walk, I followed the recipe.

Occupation is essential. And now with some pleasure I find that it's seven; and must cook dinner. Haddock and sausage meat. I think it is true that one gains a certain hold on sausage and haddock by writing them down. Virginia Woolf wrote that in her diary; I remember it because it was her last entry before she filled her pockets with stones and drowned herself in the Ouse River.

Venice. There are names about which nothing further need be said.

I landed in late morning. The sky was clear and blue, and everything appeared sharp and vivid through the plane's window: the oily green lagoon, the red-brick roofs, the sinuous forms of the islands; and in the center, like a queen, the shining bend of the Grand Canal.

I kept my hand pressed to the window the whole time we flew over the city.

"Submerged Literature" was the name of the conference that Laura had palmed off on me, citing some excuse, and I had hastened to buy a new sheath and have my hair cut, so the curls were now short, and only a couple of longer strands brushed my neck. I'd borrowed the quilted jacket, however, and at the top of the ramp, leaving behind the flight attendant's good-byes, I swam in those two sizes too large. In my pocket I clutched the hotel brochure: five stars, overlooking the lagoon, with a private dock and planters filled with pink petunias.

In a burst of enthusiasm, I had packed clothes that were too dressy. During the conference sessions, I was distracted by the sober jackets the others wore, by the solid-colored turtlenecks. I drew my coat over my clothes, embarrassed.

I envied the earnest glasses worn by Gioia, the girl who attended the conference with me, the ease with which she spoke of contemporary authors, the fact that she liked makeup.

I, on the other hand, did nothing but fill my pockets with hotel stationery, and in the morning I vied with a Neapolitan guest, the taste of toothpaste still in my mouth, to get a breakfast table overlooking the lagoon. I raced down the stairs, skirt billowing a little, and with great class beat them all and sat down at the table.

From there you could see the sun rising over San Giorgio Maggiore, the church becoming a smoke-gray silhouette against an orange backdrop. It must have been seven a.m. The prows of the moored gondolas were drenched with light, the rippling water sparkled. I stared out, cup in hand. The tea, invariably, cooled.

The organizer of the conference was Oliviero Mari, and he was tall, very tall. He popped up everywhere in the photographs at Palazzo Cini, a conspicuous plume against the background of the lagoon.

In the evening, during the dinners hosted by the publishers, he quarreled with everyone about the role of publishing houses. The *risotto al radicchio* steamed on his fork, forming vaporous rings in the air as he gestured with it. Only the final liqueur brought peace, as every matter of principle was doused in the dunked *baicoli*, the famed Venetian biscotti.

After dinner, we cleared out of the restaurant, and only Gioia and I and a guy named Marco were left. He wore a red windbreaker and had a huge camera around his neck—Silvia thought he looked like a goldfish.

We left behind the Café Florian and its orchestra, Piazza San Marco, the porticoes like enchanted grottos, and told ourselves that we would never forget those days.

Gioia, meanwhile, was taken with a young Latin teacher who persisted in showing up at the conference in a fleece vest.

Marco asked me to take a picture with him. When I said okay, we posed at the quay on the island of San Giorgio Maggiore. God, was he ever taller than me! "I wanted to take a picture with the sweetest smile at the conference," Marco said as he snapped the flash. I came out looking like a tiny dwarf, lost in the borrowed black quilted jacket, the white scarf carelessly coiled around my neck, knees clenched awkwardly.

Is that a sound coming from the other room? I put the pen down, go and check. In the kitchen, the mixture is resting in the dark. Ingredients rigorously separate—Vittorio would spread his arms smugly. I, however, would like to raise my hand to speak. "Why not mix?"

Once, by phone, Vittorio said to me, "Haven't I taught you anything?"

I often think about it, every time I give in to the same temptation of fusion, of wholly giving. I think about the way he ended that phone call. "Each of us has been left with his own flaws, apparently." I remember the patch of wall that my eyes stared at after his statement. I had the feeling that the patch of wall was staring back at me, dismayed and perhaps relieved to be just a heap of brick and plaster.

The living room is getting dark. In the distance, a pink sky skims the strip of sea visible from this window. I wait a little longer before turning on the light so that I can resume writing. In this half-light everything is suspended—I see the ferrymen who gave me their hand, saying, "Careful, madame," and I hear a concertina on a wedding couple's gondola and a small group of Americans shouting, "Hey! You there!" to attract their attention. I, who had never seen Venice before, was there too, standing at the railing of a vaporetto, staring at a small rectangular object shining in the water. It was floating, half-submerged, and had the color and wrinkled surface of a piece of aluminum foil. It must have been light, because when we cast off the moorings, the side of our boat barely touched it and it spun around a few times. It reflected a ray of sunshine more intensely, like a brief flash, then it was lost in our wake.

The last evening, the editor Elsa Carraro invited us to dinner. Palazzo Carraro was in the Cannaregio district. The facade of the Church of the Scalzi, the Ponte delle Guglie, and the Fondamenta dei Mori glided past the vaporetto's windows. The canals were dark pools.

When the door opened, we found ourselves facing a large marble staircase. Antique maps of Venice hung on the walls of the entryway.

"The canal in red, you see"—Oliviero Mari pointed on the map—"it was to divert the waters of the Sile and Muson Rivers from the lagoon . . . However, the best part is farther on, they're from the early nineteenth century."

"What?"

"The two gondolas in the side alcoves. Let's hurry, so we can all go in together."

Bewildered, I stumbled on a step. Someone snickered behind me.

When we arrived, there were already a hundred guests and the staff of a chaotic catering service. The guests were distinguished and famished. When the battle for food was over, they clustered in small knots, wineglasses in hand, red-faced, trying to drown out the others by speaking louder than necessary. A middle-aged Slavic singer intoned improbable dirges accompanied by a harp. She had an enormous bosom, and many eyes focused on it.

"I've never seen a house with so many books." Gioia sighed meanwhile, indicating the bookshelves lining the walls and stairs.

In a corner, a man in his forties turned on the stereo and started swaying his hips, his eyes closed. He was big and graceful; when he opened his eyes, I saw that they were a clear, dull green.

"That's Damiano Certi," Gioia informed me. "He has an independent publishing house."

Shortly thereafter, a number of people surrounded him, dancing disjointedly, still holding their glasses.

"Dear God!" I laughed. "They're older than my parents!"

It was then that someone took me by the elbow. "Miss . . ."

I jumped. He was a tall, thin man. He wore thick glasses with black oval frames, which distorted his facial features.

He pointed to a door. "Have you seen the most interesting room in the house?"

The room was hung with paintings of nudes: scenes of autoeroticism, sadism, the humiliating nakedness of elderly people. Angular lines, edgy brushstrokes, black paint dripped onto the canvas.

In the middle of the wall, a man and a woman, frontal. Naked, each with a hand on the other's genitals, their eyes morbidly fixed on the viewer, as if inviting him to participate. Shocked, I recognized the woman in the painting as the hostess.

"Please, come this way." The man headed toward the small balcony, I followed him.

"See that small building with the triple lancet window full of flowers? That's the home of Tintoretto."

"Really?"

He lit a cigarette. Two men passed by, chatting beneath the balcony.

"Whenever Elsa invites me to dinner, I come here to get a look at that building. Ah, Tintoretto's painting, so frenzied . . ."

I too stared at the distant window, my mind still on the nude image of Elsa Carraro. Who was the man in the painting?

"Forgive me, professional bias," he added soon afterward, smoothing his hair. "I edit the art history series at P. Editions."

He held out his hand, told me his name.

"Why is Tintoretto's painting frenzied?" I asked.

"It's not easy to search for the divine in what is human, is it?" he replied. Then he turned to me, his eyes seeming to go right through me. I crossed my arms to cover my breasts.

"And you," he asked, "what are you searching for?"

"I don't think I know." I heard my voice come out shrill.

"When I was young, I would spend whole afternoons in a café at Campo San Barnaba with my friends." He pointed to a distant square somewhere in the city. "Whole afternoons swapping our art history books, planning great things, one with a passion for sculpture, another for architecture. We lived swept along by our utopias . . ."

I thought about my adolescence, about strolling up and down Via Sparano. About the kids from the working-class neighborhoods who, as a prank at Carnival time, squirted us with white foam sold in spray cans, and how we couldn't say a word.

Maybe that's why, when he asked me, "Do you have a passion?"

"Writing," I said.

"Writing . . . damn. Poetry? Stories?"

"I'm writing a novel." I told him the title, *The Perfect Almond Tree*, and the name of the protagonist, Silvia, my face hot, embarrassed because I had never told anyone.

The man was studying me now with a sort of adoration in his eyes as I stammered out the reason I was writing the story. He asked me, "Do you really believe in that final message?"

He moved closer, I backed away. I caught sight of guests passing by in the hallway, I searched for an excuse to go back in. Nevertheless, I didn't do it. I just needed to talk that night. Because that night Venice was a mirror in a fairy tale, the kind you look in to choose who to be and by magic you are. Because I was in that magnificent palazzo, among people who seemed remarkable, and it didn't matter in what sense: they were dazzling. Because that night I was simply a ship that has been cast loose from its moorings and, once out to sea, is finally awash in its element: there is only water, water that does not require, water that does not scrutinize. Home is far away, so you can be whatever you want to be, perhaps what you are.

"Your left eye looks wistful," he said, switching to the familiar form of address. "Here"—he brushed a strand of hair back from my forehead—"the right one is smaller, more guarded, more wary. The difference is incredible: the right one watches, the left one dreams. Yes, undoubtedly it's dreaming."

I began to sweat.

"Don't be embarrassed, they're both beautiful, but be careful about the left one, because it's a siren's song."

"So much the worse for others." I laughed with feigned unconcern.

"I'm not so sure."

"It's just that I feel split in two, always," I admitted, then.

He gave me the satisfied look of an animal that has flushed out its prey.

"Split in two? Maybe you are one but trying desperately to be someone else. Or . . ."

"Or?"

"Or you're a bit schizophrenic!"

It was the violence of that term, the obscenity of the laughter that accompanied it, that woke me up.

"It's late, we booked the vaporetto for this time, the others will be leaving without me."

I went back inside. I said good-bye to him. He followed me down the hall, tried to stop me. He even came into the coatroom.

"Excuse me," I said, my voice shaking. He tried to take my hand, I twisted out of his grip. He gave me a moist kiss on the cheek—it made me think of a snail. He handed me his card.

"If you feel like it tonight, call me. We can stroll around Venice."

"Good night."

"Why are you dashing off? You're acting like little Lilì! Slow down! Where are you running to, *petite Lilì*?" He laughed.

"I have no idea who little Lilì is!" I admitted, muttering under my breath as I left Palazzo Carraro.

Only much, much later would I discover who she was.

On the quay I ran into Gioia.

"Antonia! There you are, finally! I couldn't find you, the vaporetto left without us!"

I told her everything in a rush, apologizing again and again.

"Don't worry, those people are here. They'll give us a ride on the speedboat, they're staying at the same hotel."

I climbed aboard. Who "those people" were didn't interest me, all I wanted was to get back to my room and forget how ashamed of myself I was. But I noticed him as soon as we sat down. I looked up, and there he was in front of me, Vittorio.

5

Day Two.

I was surprised when I entered the kitchen and found the bowl with the mixture; I had almost forgotten.

"You started it!" Anna said, satisfied, then turned back to ironing my dress.

I've been invited to the theater. A guy, an actor, promised me that after the show he'd get me into the dressing rooms.

It's important to move on, accept every invitation, let them pursue you. Let them make promises, pretend you believe them. Seduce in order to feel like more than a ghost.

"It's good for you to go out," said Anna, firmly pressing out a crease.

"Right."

He'll come to pick me up, standing there stiffly in an elegant coat, I can already picture him. He'll buy me a drink in the lobby. I'll eat and drink, moving my knees away, then touching under the table, like a child, while he gets up every minute to greet someone. During the show, he'll turn often to look at me, to see how much I'm enjoying it—him too. He'll make a move, placing a hand lightly on my arm, I'll move my arm away.

"There." Anna showed me the result of her work, pleased with herself.

I'll have him lead me backstage, up the stairs, past walls hung with posters of old shows. I'll appear extremely excited to meet the actors. I'll say, "Great performance" as I shake their hands.

"I'll hang it outside the closet so it won't get crushed."

We'll get back in the car, he'll ask me, "Shall we take a ride?" and I'll say, "Thanks, but I'm tired, it's late." I'll add an "I had a nice time" when we get to the house and he shuts off the engine, turns sideways in the driver's seat and fondles my coat; I'll bolt out of the car, fumble with the keys to the front door; in the elevator, I won't look at myself in the mirror.

"No, go ahead and put it in the closet. I'll take care of it later."

The truth is, Anna, that I can't do it.

Because Vittorio even robbed me of the joy of going to the theater, buying a dress, putting on nail polish; and though I'd like to, I really can't forgive him for the fact that I feel nauseated just thinking about getting in a car that isn't his, with its CD player that played in fits and starts and the books stuffed in the glove compartment . . .

"Shall we follow the recipe?"

Day Two: Stir the mixture and cover with aluminum foil.

Mix. Mix. Mix. (No, Vittorio, you haven't taught me anything.)

Although the mixture was rather thick, the wooden spoon, stirring, formed concentric circles: the circles of a tree trunk.

Gioia had just said to me and the Latin teacher, "Don't you find the bark of this tree beautiful?"

It was midafternoon, and we were in the gardens of the Palazzo dei Congressi, on the island of San Giorgio Maggiore. It was still daylight, but the light was subtle, the kind that begins to fall slantingly, lengthening the shadows. Yes, the bark was beautiful, and I looked at Gioia with gratitude, because she had noticed the tree, because she had made me see it.

My phone rang, I stepped away to answer it. "Yes, Laura, everything is going well." I followed the pathway and came to the water's edge. When I'd said good-bye, I stopped to take it all in. There was peace, there was silence, the languor of Venice was everywhere. In the distance, Marco, lying belly up on the grass, was taking photographs. Of what? Of things that only he could see.

It was the last day. Here it was, Venice, a picture-postcard city that only revealed its facades, as if it weren't three-dimensional. Yet I had entered its doors, its hotels, its palazzi. Finally, there had been something that wasn't meant to be just looked at.

"So, what do you think of our time here?"

Vittorio was not one to ask whether he was disturbing you by suddenly coming up behind you in a park.

He wore a white shirt and a dark suit. He looked elegant and seemed unusually cheerful.

"It's been very lovely. Strange but wonderful." I glanced around. Where was Gioia?

"Didn't your colleague come to the sessions?" I managed.

"Damiano? I don't know, he too must have been 'swamped.'"

"By last night's alcohol, maybe."

Could his smile be any broader?

The night before, in the speedboat, we had not spoken. If he'd recognized me, he hadn't shown any sign of it. But then he'd been pretty drunk. He was sitting next to Damiano Certi, they were whispering.

Somewhere along the way, the boat had stalled. The pilot had tried to restart the engine, but his efforts were met by a less-than-comforting whining. We were all quiet, apprehensive, the lagoon even more silent than we were.

"Shit!" our pilot had blurted out at a certain point, before slumping down in his seat.

Vittorio had stood up, struggling to keep his balance. "Great," he said. "That says it all about the situation we're in, publishers, editors, and journalists!"

"Well, at least we're all in the same boat!" Damiano had thrown in.

They had kept us entertained with their banter until another speedboat arrived to transfer us.

The second trip was quieter: Damiano slept, in an alcoholic stupor, Vittorio sat in front of me. The boat raced like mad toward the lagoon.

"You'd think we were Lara Croft!" Gioia had quipped. We'd laughed. Vittorio had looked over at us, I'd looked straight at him. He pulled a black wool cap out of his pocket and put it on, holding my gaze; he had thick salt-and-pepper eyebrows, bags under eyes that had turned a pale gray-blue. I was the one to look away.

"Is it really that obvious that we're a bunch of degenerates?" he asked me in the park of the Palazzo dei Congressi.

Degenerates, I noted. It conveyed the idea.

"The truth?"

"Sure."

"I never saw so many crazies together!"

I bit my tongue. But Vittorio laughed heartily. "Why do you say that?" he asked me. And he wouldn't leave me alone until he was satisfied with my answer.

While I stumbled over my words, his eyes were on mine, first one, then the other, then down to my lips, tracing a triangular pattern. Or was it my nose he was looking at? I covered it with my hand, briefly, that nose that was too long, and kept quiet.

Vittorio looked away.

"So you're a journalist?"

"But I don't want to be a journalist."

"Why?"

"Because the preceding day's newspapers become scrap paper."

I looked up at him to see the effect of my words. Vittorio lit a cigarette with no expression.

"You should read *Late Summer Song*, I'm sure you'd like it. It's a book we published last year. It's a story about a retired professor. One day . . ."

Vittorio went on talking, and I was drawn into his circle. Attracted by his magnetic gestures, by his way of shaking his head when the talk grew intense, by the mark he had on his skin, beneath his right eye; by the full lips that I didn't want to look at, yet kept looking at.

Within a few minutes an idiotic grin had spread over my face.

"So you're in Milan, for now," he said suddenly.

"Yes." I tucked a strand of hair behind my ear, crossed my legs.

"What's your name?"

"Antonia."

"Antonia," he repeated. A childlike joy appeared on his face.

The light in the park became more docile. Vittorio glanced at his watch, took one last drag on the cigarette he'd just lit, and tossed it into the water. I felt a vague disappointment at the carelessness of his act.

"It's cold," he said, rubbing his arms. "Shall we go back to the hall?"

He walked ahead of me, and I saw that there was a rolled-up newspaper sticking out of his back pocket.

"With none other than the playboy of the group," Marco said, seeing us come back in together. "I thought you were less predictable."

At the end of the conference, we took a group photo. While we were asked to smile for the camera, I caught Vittorio in the act as he pointed me out to a friend from across the room.

He came over again.

"I have to go back to Milan with the others." I held back, playing hard to get.

He handed me his business card. "Write me, tell me about yourself, if you like."

One night, much later, in his bed, I asked him about that day.

"Remember that?"

"No."

"Why not?"

"We were introduced."

"We were not introduced! You're so pigheaded!" I went to give him a kiss on the forehead, but my naked body got tangled up in the sheets. "You stopped me, you started a conversation. And you even pointed me out to your friend. Do you at least remember why?"

"Who knows? I must have thought you were attractive."

"Hmm."

"Right, I thought, 'She's attractive.' Can we go to sleep?" and he closed his eyes without waiting for an answer.

6

Sunday in Milan. Ecological marathons, traffic blocked off, sleepy neighborhoods. Sidewalks like empty trampolines: nowhere to perform on a Sunday morning.

"How beautiful Milan is without cars!" they said on the radio. I switched it off.

The only remaining sound was the clatter of the pots, stacked one inside the other, that I was trying to separate, squatting over my ankles, head inside the kitchen cabinet.

Back home, my family must have already finished dinner. I could picture my mother clearing the table, my uncle holding on to his glass: "What the hell is your hurry?"

Certainly my father must already be on his way to the sofa, Grandpa lighting the burner under the coffee. Grandma, with a few gestures, would be directing operations.

Meanwhile, I added salt to the cooking water and looked out the window. My neighbor was there at her window, I waved hello to her, but maybe she didn't realize it was meant for her, she didn't respond.

I turned on the computer, set it beside the placemat.

By now they must have split up, I imagined: men in the den, dozing in front of the TV, waiting for the game. Mama and Grandma, sitting on the living room couch, would have picked up their knitting. My aunt would still be sweeping in the kitchen. "Ida, come inside, we already cleaned up, Caterina will do the rest tomorrow!" Grandma must be shouting to her. But Ida has to wipe the dishcloth over the burners, she must remove the deposits, make the stove sparkle. Then she will light a cigarette and smoke it, looking out the window. There she is, her curly red hair barely stirred by the breeze as she inhales and blows away the smoke, her eyes gazing at the deserted Sunday afternoon street. I know her thoughts are flying at that moment. If I were there, I imagined, I'd go and sit beside her, and our thoughts placed together would indeed make a deafening noise. A voice would be calling her again, one last illusion of freedom would make her smile faintly before returning to the living room.

As a young girl, when she went shopping with Grandma, Ida would take off her shoes in the street: she'd abandon first one, then a few blocks later the other. My grandmother would only notice it when they got home, and she had to walk back through the whole city to find them. No matter how old you get, some things you never stop doing.

I began surfing the net senselessly. I typed "Vittorio Solmani," deleted it before pressing "Enter." I could have looked at his business card, written him an e-mail. What had Marco called him? The Don Juan of the conference. Or had he said playboy? I moved the computer away.

After dinner, I lay down on the couch with a book, plunged into silence. Something that would not have been possible at my house. Perhaps, therefore, as I read, I seemed to breathe deeply, and the image of the ball of yarn that Mama had certainly let fall to her feet—thick wool, orange, will she manage to finish the sweater this time before the season changes?—and their chatter about the latest recipes found in the paper became more blurred . . . How often I had dozed off listening to them. Then the shouts from the other room—"Goal!"—would abruptly wake me. Or more often the swearing for a missed penalty kick.

There it is, that queasy feeling, right in the stomach.

I would shut myself up in my grandfather's study, open his antiquated books. But just as a sentence I'd read seemed to turn a light on in my head, and as the whole room, by contrast, became a blurry image, a final affront found its way in despite the closed door.

"Shitty referee! He's been bought!" A chair would crash, a fist angrily pounded the table. No reaction came from the living room, they went on knitting and chatting. I would close the book and dream of escaping to where life did not have the depressing background of a soccer commentary.

> From: antonia@libero.it
> To: vittorioso@gmail.com
> Subject: Tram stop: XXIV Maggio
>
> Hello, Vittorio,
>
> I don't know if you remember me. We spoke on the island of San Giorgio Maggiore, you recommended I read *Late Summer Song*.
>
> I wanted to tell you that I bought it that same day. Then I took my last vaporetto ride, got on the train, and Venice disappeared. I had a strange sensation, as if it were the end of something and the beginning of something

else. If you've ever had that feeling, you know it's not sad: beginnings always end up being the best part. Anyway, I devoured the book on the train to Milan, unable to look up even for a moment, and then on the subway, with my carry-on constantly tipping over onto the other passengers' legs, and then again on the tram that took me home . . . I was so engrossed that when I heard a voice say, "End of the line," I realized that home was now several stops back.

Because it was talking about Venice, that book, even though it was Amsterdam. And about me, having gone away, even though the protagonist's name was Farrow and he was a professor with prostatitis.

"'Well, you went away. Is it any wonder? Loss is the essence of life,' said Bill under his old cap. Meanwhile in Amsterdam, the snow had completely melted, it was April, and someone was arriving at the station with a large suitcase. A ray of light filtered into what had been my room."

And so everything became lighter, even Milan, at night, at the wrong stop, with a carry-on that was heavier and heavier, a stocking with a run in it, and hungry enough to eat a horse.

How astonishing.

So, in short, thank you.

Antonia ("that one" from the seminar in Venice)

As I pressed the "Send" key, I thought, After all, what can happen?

THE PERFECT ALMOND TREE
JOYFUL FOR SOME UNKNOWN KINDNESS

The village of San F. was sun drenched when Silvia walked through it, late in the morning. Along the streets, large fishing nets were spread out to dry on plastic chairs.

In Silvia's head, a guitar played something cheerful, her feet glided first right, then left, as in a tango.

The path to the beach descended steeply. The uneven paving stones made Franco the postman bounce on the seat of his bicycle as he passed Silvia, bumping along clumsily and punctuating the morning with cries of "ouch" and "ow," and countdowns to retirement.

For Silvia, however, the stones seemed to soften under her feet. "Tell us, signorina, where can we bring you today?" they asked, and the balconies, with their cascades of geraniums, replied, "Silvia goes to the beach every morning, when will you ever learn?"

In her head, a flute began to play.

The bicycle leaning against the wall spoke up. "May I have the honor of accompanying you, Signorina Silvia?"

She made a little bow and continued on.

In the butchers' doorways, children swung from the cables of the awnings—they did not take their eyes off her. The rotisserie chickens seemed to rotate to the music's rhythm.

At the bar, which was also a tobacconist, newsstand, and sundries shop selling shampoo, cotton balls, and yellowed postcards, old men were gathered around the card table.

"Good morning! Good morning! Good morning!" Silvia greeted them. They raised their heads from the cards, stopped their squabbling, and winked at her. Then the maracas joined in to set the rhythm in her head, and it was all one big concert down to the sea.

Approaching the beach, the cubes of bare concrete multiplied: they were houses that had been under construction for years, which some impromptu developer from the interior had had built and which had been seized by judicial authorities; forgotten there, while the money was better spent on a parking lot that filled up in the summertime, with a miniature blue train that carried people to the shore. So the houses in San F. were left like toothless mouths, their windows without panes overlooking the sea.

The pastel pink house, however, was beautiful, dilapidated, and smelling of salt air. It was the last house in town, already leaning toward the shore. A huge cactus covered half the facade, it looked like a sculpture of candelabras balanced one on top of another; in contrast, the green shutters on which Silvia knocked, three times, every morning were miniscule.

She picked up the pinwheels left on the steps, stuck them in the window planter boxes, and blew on them with all the breath she had until they started spinning. Then she placed her mouth at an opening in the shutters and shouted, "Engine running, Mr. Amilcare! Ready to set sail!"

She could hear the old man shuffling behind the door—the smell of coffee?—then the ritual question, uttered in the hoarse voice of old age: "How is the weather out there, Captain Silvia?"

Silvia pretended to look around, assessing the clarity of the sky and, with a saliva-moistened finger, the wind direction. "As beautiful as Americaaa!" she shouted, and resumed her race toward the sea, with violins and maracas and even a trumpet playing, and behind her, old Amilcare's laughter and the pinwheels on his windowsill spinning crazily.

7

From: vittorioso@gmail.com
To: antonia@libero.it
Subject: Re: Tram stop: XXIV Maggio

Antonia, really "that" Antonia! What a wonderful surprise!

I'm glad: that you liked the book, that you wrote to me, that good old Farrow alleviated your nostalgia. We don't often meet people capable of being astonished and of communicating that astonishment with your spontaneity. But I had already sensed that as we were talking in Venice and my first impressions are (almost) never wrong.

If you like, I'll give you a few books of ours, provided it won't affect your rail and tram mobility.

By the way, there's a fantastic restaurant near the Piazza XXIV Maggio stop, if you're still hungry enough to eat a horse, we could go together, that way I'll have a chance to apologize for your misadventures (I still can't make up my mind whether there's a bit of irony in your "so thank you" . . .).

I might even teach you how not to let your suitcase fall on other people's feet in the subway—it's a type of asana that requires a great deal of discipline, in fact.

Let me know about dinner, if you feel like it.
XXX,
V.
P.S. If anyone owes the other hours of astonishment, it's me, to you.

At the planetarium there was a nighttime lecture on love and constellations: "Eurydice, Andromeda, and Others: Eternal Love Told by the Constellations."

There were about thirty of us, waiting behind the high fence enclosing the gardens. Wrought iron curlicues against the dark green of the night.

We proceeded in silence when the custodian unbolted the gate, forming an orderly line along the path. A shaft of light from the streetlamp fell on the gravel, making it gleam with a whiteness so beautiful that I bent to pick some up, as if it were made of seashells.

Night birds were singing. We opened and closed the clips of our purses, and were already studying the sky, impatient. The subtle sound of a fountain trickling in the park.

"Five minutes," a guard said.

A little girl looked up at her grandfather, he winked at her; the girl took his hand and prepared to wait.

That night at the planetarium, we learned that the word "desire" derives from "de" and "sidera," stars, and that desires are something unattainable, like the stars themselves. When they fall, however, they appear to come closer to us, and so even desires come to meet us halfway. That is why it is believed that shooting stars fulfill them.

We learned a lot more, which we have now forgotten. But the truth is that when we sat down inside the planetarium and all the lights went out and there was only a sky full of stars overhead—so many we couldn't imagine they could all fit in there—all at once our breath caught and we lost the perception of things, of where we were.

"Holy Christ," was all Gioia said, and I shushed her for breaking the silence.

As we went out, we stumbled along, dazed.

Looking for a tram to go home, we couldn't utter a word other than "beautiful."

"You know what I desire?" Gioia mumbled. "A man to go to the planetarium with. Who understands."

"Yeah," I replied, but maybe Gioia had already gotten off at her stop, and the only ones left on the tram were me, the driver, and the approaching dawn.

Vittorio Solmani would be horrified at the very idea, I thought, but I didn't say it.

> From: antonia@libero.it
> To: vittorioso@gmail.com
> Subject: Genoa station
>
> Hi, Vittorio,
>
> I hope you don't mind that I changed my stop, but staying still is not one of my greatest virtues. I never know where to lay an egg, to quote my grandmother. In fact, this weekend I'm going away. Why don't *you* astonish me, by joining me? In Porto Venere, Sunday, for lunch. Then we can come back together.
>
> Antonia

"You know what my Greek literature professor always said?" I winked at Silvia. "Antonia, look how the gods have fallen!"

Silvia laughed.

"You and I don't let ourselves be had so easily!" I added.

I turned on some music, how nice my living room was that evening.

"Do you think the beige suit will do?"

8

Tell the woman he picked up at the party on the river, the blonde to whom he offered a glass of wine while he rattled off the script of his daily obsessions to make her laugh. Tell the pretty blonde with the narrow-waisted red designer jacket, who is now brushing her hair on the edge of Vittorio's bed and will soon dash off to the office, leaving him with a "See you" like a worldly sophisticate.

Tell her that I walked in that room, barefoot. I made the bed while Vittorio was in the shower. I looked at the books he had on the shelves, not daring to touch them. I saw him come back into the room, wearing his bathrobe, his hair wet; he would wipe his face with his sleeve and, in a hoarse morning voice, with his soft "r," ask me, "Dressed already?"

Ask the blonde with the ponytail who smiles coldly as they talk, her back ramrod straight, who will now go around saying that she fucked Vittorio Solmani; that's what she'll say, no more, no less.

Does she know that Vittorio always buys fresh pasta from the same woman? That his favorite T-shirt is red, with the logo of a philosophy journal on it? That part of his shirt is always hanging out of his pants? That he can't dance (the night he tried, at my place, we laughed so hard it hurt), that he adds rosemary to every dish, that he has awful slippers?

I would have cut off all my hair for him. Tell that to the blonde who now plucks hers from the brush, annoyed.

In that same room, Vittorio, naked, would open the closet and choose which shirt to wear. His back to me. Sitting on the bed, with eyeliner already on my eyes and my bag on my shoulder, I followed the line of his backbone. Morning was slowly moving into the room: a triangle of light formed on the checkered floor, between the bed and the closet, it fell on Vittorio's bare foot.

And now I find a photograph of him in a newspaper, and I wonder, "Has he dyed his hair?"

I go into the kitchen, looking for the cake mixture. Give me something to do tonight, Padre Pio, I'm tired of sobbing into a pillow. Does that count as a prayer?

But not even the concoction is my friend today.

Day Three: Let the mixture rest without stirring.

Sometimes you just can't do anything about it. You have to wait.

Why is it that at some point our emotions take an unexpected turn? All of a sudden, they derail.

In the train that brought me back to Milan that Sunday night, I tried for a long time to get them back on track, but they had already set off.

The window's glass stubbornly reflected my image, the outline of my disheveled hair, the protective light of the compartment, the sleepy surrender of the other passengers. The nocturnal landscape was nothing but an intermittence of lights flying past against a dark backdrop.

Vittorio had not come. After all, my invitation had been absurd. A challenge, a way to put him to the test, to make him take it back. "If anyone owes the other hours of astonishment, it's me, to you." You shouldn't write things like that. Because someone, reading them, might widen her eyes, linger a beat longer over those unexpected words, repeat them to herself at dull moments of the day.

I was sure that those words were just bait for him to hook another one of his catches. I'm no fool to be bamboozled by such trite clichés, I told myself as I read those words again, and if I really astonished him, he'll come to Porto Venere. Vittorio had not come.

I imagined him sitting next to me on that train. My body would not have been turned completely toward the window, huddled up. I would have hidden my profile from him, since I am somewhat ashamed of it; he would have talked and talked, in his knowing way, and maybe at some point he would have fallen silent, he would have caressed my cheek and said, "If anyone owes the other hours of astonishment . . ."

But Vittorio had not come.

I had unmasked him. I'd done well, I hadn't swallowed his bait, not me. I could be proud of myself.

But what was that emptiness in my chest, that sense of something lost, of the last day of summer?

What nonsense, I kept telling myself, it's got nothing to do with him. It's only a tendency to fantasize. It's only a void that needs to be filled. It's exhaustion from the long day. It's being homesick, a little lonely. This sadness is not about him: it's the train traveling through the night, it's the landscape that cannot be seen, it's the absent gaze of the man sitting across from me, it's the cell phone that hasn't vibrated for hours, it's the faint whisper of magazine pages being turned in the rapt silence of the compartment . . .

As the train carried me back to Milan, I was swerving off the right track.

9

Meanwhile, Silvia was growing up. Between the lines that I was writing about her—late at night, squinting myopically at the small screen of a laptop—and all around me, as if she were real. She would suddenly appear on the subway platform, playfully peeping out from behind a newspaper; she'd wait for me at the supermarket door to take the other handle of the shopping bag and share the burden. We crossed the street like that, joined by a plastic bag always about to split open, and she talked and talked and talked. I dragged her along when cars failed to slow down, and she pointed to the striped crosswalks, pouting. Then she started hopping on them, one foot for each stripe; if she missed one, she had to go back to the starting point.

Silvia was twenty years old, young as a child and mature as a grown woman. She suffered from Down syndrome, "but that's just a detail," as she put it. Who knows who had taught her to say that. Silvia, plainly speaking, had almond-shaped eyes because she was born under an almond tree. That's how her father, Ruggero, had explained it to her.

"Children are born under trees, and every tree determines the shape or color of their eyes. Your mother, for example, was born under a chestnut tree, because her eyes are the color of chestnuts, and even have their shape a little if you look closely. I was born under a pine tree—see the green of my iris? And you, like your friends from the Association, were born under an almond tree."

"The one we have in the courtyard?"

"Right under your window."

She had a mind of her own, Silvia did, and a primitive, elementary joy; maybe that's why I couldn't do without her.

The truth was that she didn't wonder what to do with her hands when someone spoke to her, or how to position her arms, or where to look. She didn't ask herself, Should I stand up straight? How will my voice sound?

A terrible thing, this matter of the voice. The fact that none of us hears it the way it sounds to others creates a divide between everything that we are: are we the voice we ourselves hear or the one others hear? How strange life is, you can't help but be perplexed by it.

But not Silvia, Silvia did not experience this perplexity; in her, life was immediate. In Silvia, it was as if the inner and outer voices coincided and there's no denying that was a form of happiness. At least until she fell in love with Antonio. Love upsets everything, damn it!

10

"I need to keep moving from house to house. After a couple of years at most, I have to relocate."

Vittorio had taken me to a cocktail lounge in Milan, with huge chandeliers and roomy white sofas, more like beds. Maybe that was the impression I had given him, of a girl who liked trendy spots.

"Shall we lie down?" he joked, pointing to the red cushions scattered on the sofas. I didn't get the joke.

"It's just that there are already certainties in my life, work, for example," he explained, "and I need to know that not everything has been predetermined, that there is room for change."

"A bit demanding, a move every two years!"

"Actually, I have very few things with me, by now I've planned it out!"

A young man came to take our orders. I hesitated.

"Do you have soft drinks?"

Vittorio laughed. "A soft drink?"

"I don't drink." I shrugged.

"You at least smoke, I hope!"

"No. For that matter, I don't drink coffee either!"

"I don't believe I've ever met anyone who didn't do any of those three things!"

I ordered a fruity cocktail as Vittorio shook his head, enjoying himself.

We weren't supposed to have gone there that night. He'd asked me out, I had rerouted him to the former wool mill, where I'd been with my friends for a concert. I didn't want to be alone with him.

"Just to be clear!" I'd explained to Gioia.

"What is there to be clear about?"

I had no answer.

But then Vittorio had been late. Throughout the whole concert, I'd kept an eye on the entrance while struggling with my skirt that persistently rode up my thighs. Then a text message appeared: *I'm out here, I have no idea where to park. I'll wait for you.*

He'd done as he'd wanted.

"However"—he took off his glasses and placed them on the table—"I have some habits that are sacred. Four o'clock coffee, for example, is obligatory."

"No matter where you are?"

"No matter where. Like a Muslim kneels at the call of the muezzin. Movies on Monday nights, as well. Dinner with friends on Tuesday, a Sunday morning fruit shake . . ." He listed them, pleased with himself.

"And these habits may not be disrupted?"

"No."

"You'd sooner move to a new house?"

"Yep!"

I looked at his hands. They were nice, but not graceful. Suited for the handlebars of a motorcycle.

"When they're interrupted, I feel disoriented. But I also need to know that around these certainties there is a world that can be reinvented each day. Freedom, the most beautiful word," he concluded, spreading his arms.

"Freedom to be a slave to your habits?"

He put his glasses back on. He spread his legs, leaned toward me (lucky him, knowing how to get comfortable on those sofas, I thought).

"Freedom to choose what to be a slave to." He frowned. "Freedom is not a boundless space in which we can't even glimpse a horizon. That's not the freedom that I believe in, at least."

"Ma'am, your coat is on the floor," a waitress said. I bent to pick it up, embarrassed. Now I was beginning to drop things.

"Besides, you don't ask for freedom, but for some appearance of freedom. Emil Cioran *docet*." He ate an olive and spit the pit out in his napkin.

He held out the bowl, offering me one. The idea of spitting out a pit in front of a man whom I barely knew embarrassed me. I shook my finger no.

The waiter arrived with our orders. Vittorio took off his glasses again, exposing the blue of his eyes, and we toasted.

From the window you could see the Arch of Peace.

"Shall we walk a bit, afterward?" I asked.

"Don't you like this place?"

"Yes, of course, I just feel like taking a little walk."

"I can't imagine where we could go. In Milan you don't walk, in Milan you move from one point to another with an objective."

He looked at me for a moment or two, smiled with a certain gentleness. I rubbed the back of my neck.

"And you?" he asked, spearing an olive with a toothpick.

"What about me?"

"Do you have a boyfriend?"

"Why do you ask that as if you'd been talking about your girlfriend?"

"I was talking about my relationship with freedom."

"That's not a woman."

"But it's a love."

"I have a mole, and when I was a child, I decided that the man who noticed it would be the man of my life."

"The man of my life!" he echoed me. "It's been years since I've heard anyone say that!"

"A lack of romantic imagination, perhaps," I parried in my defense. The words tumbled out in a rush, tripping over themselves.

Vittorio took a sip of his drink.

"Is it in such a private place, your mole?"

"No, it's visible to anyone, theoretically; in actuality only a keen eye can spot it—it's a detail reserved for noble souls!"

"Is that so? I'll have to look for it, then."

He leaned on the table, pretending to study me closely.

"You wouldn't find it."

"No, I guess not." For a moment he seemed thrown by my gibe. "And someone has been more worthy than me?"

"A man noticed it, yes, the first time we went out. We were together for many years. We were happy together. We wanted to get married, but then things turned out differently . . ."

"How old were you?"

"Twenty-two."

"Good thing you didn't marry."

"Why?"

"What do you mean, why? At twenty-two!"

"Who knows."

Music drifted through the lounge.

"A mole, imagine that!" And he burst into one of his beautiful smiles that lit up his face. He began moving his head and his foot to the rhythm of the music.

He kept glancing at me delightedly; I couldn't help but smile at him, even if I didn't mean to. I absolutely didn't mean to.

"What, you're even leaving the fruit drink?"

"I don't feel like any more."

When we left the club, we strolled through Milan's cold streets, and he acted as my guide. He knew the history of every monument, every piazza, every district.

"How do you know all these things?"

"It's my city."

It had stopped raining shortly before, and it seemed like Milan was sighing—one of those deep sighs breathed at the end of the day, the instant before falling asleep.

Vittorio went on enumerating dates and names, the illuminated shop windows seemed so trivial in comparison that they slipped by without rousing any desires.

I didn't know what to say and just listened. I tried to think of questions to ask him, but I couldn't come up with any. Of topics to introduce, but nothing came to mind. I walked along veering slightly, something I always did. When for a moment I found myself almost bumping into him, I felt like staying close to him. Would he ever look at me?

He had lent me his gloves. With my hands in my pockets so he wouldn't see me, I rubbed my thumb and forefinger together, to feel their texture. It was a rough wool.

Suddenly he stopped and fell silent. Was it really "Bastard" I read on his leather jacket?

He pulled out an eyeglass cloth and wiped his lenses.

I glanced around, casting about for something to say. But any idea that came to me seemed stupid compared to his discourses.

"Do you mind if I have another cigarette?" he asked, breaking the silence.

He seemed disappointed by my lack of conversation.

"No, why should I?"

He leaned against a doorway to smoke, a few feet away from me. I felt under scrutiny. "Is the young lady tongue-tied?"

I didn't respond.

"I'll take you home, then."

I stood alone in the middle of the street, confused. I looked at the sky.

"Say something, Antonia, say something. You do have a tongue, don't you?"

"For the Greeks, the moon was a girl who rode across the sky on a silver chariot drawn by white horses," I said.

Vittorio blew out the smoke abruptly, it was like a snort. I was silent.

"What's your last name?" he asked, reading the names on the entry panel when we got to my house.

I pointed to the buzzer.

"Lucida Handwriting?"

"What?"

"The font you used. For the name." A cloud of steam drifted out of his mouth.

He moved closer, I pretended to look at my name on the buzzer.

"I don't know, I don't remember . . ."

He slipped a glove off my hand to take it back, thought better of it. "Keep them, go on, I have others." He gave it to me.

"Are you throwing down the gauntlet like in the eighteenth century?" I joked.

"The eighteenth century?"

"Yes, I meant . . ."

Vittorio's face descended on mine, lips parted.

I turned my face to avoid him, humiliated by the correction. So he took my face in both his hands and tried again to kiss me. I responded shyly, then broke away.

"I want to see you again," he said in a languid voice, his hands already reaching.

"It's late, time to get some sleep," I said, restraining his hands.

The moonlight fell vertically on us. Vittorio shoved me against the door, and we kissed for a long time.

I remained sitting at the kitchen table for an hour, my coat still on. When I stood up, I said to myself, "Good thing I don't like him."

11

To return. From a journey, from a dream, to return from a love affair. You've landed, the flight is over. You can unfasten your seat belt—assuming you had the foresight to use it—gather up your carry-on bag, go down the ramp that leads you to the ground, avoid looking at the flight attendant who thanks you for having chosen that flight; get off, eyes lowered.

Day Four: Continue to let the mixture rest.

Don't give in to the temptation to mix. Wait for time to pass.
 Tonight I went out on the terrace, the city slept. I sat on the porch swing and looked up. I could see only three stars, Venus, and the Big Dipper that darkness was nibbling at.
 I rocked and the sky, viewed like that, swung back and forth.
 Maybe if I keep looking, I told myself, if I look more closely, maybe I'll find some meaning. But there isn't any, there simply isn't, just as the stars in the planetarium are no longer there; what swallowed them up? There is only this sky, which is merely a lid after all, which for one night, one night only, lifted.

And in my anger I rocked harder, faster and faster, and the lid swung but remained impassive. It wasn't even out of anger that I sped up; it was just a way of saying no. There was nothing I could do, but at least I had to say that my response was a no.

The scent of jasmine filled the air. In spite of everything, it was sweetly fragrant. I looked at the plant, and its flowers were tiny white stars in the night.

That time at the planetarium, remember, Antonia? How can you lose a night of a thousand stars? How can you lose something so irreversibly?

The past leaves us exiles, searching for stars in jasmine flowers.

I had packed two fuchsia-colored carry-ons, and I'd left for Milan. In the belief that those elegant buildings would be a guarantee of happiness.

"What are you going to do in Milan? Be a journalist?"

I didn't know.

It seemed that there was nothing consistent, nothing conclusive that could be said about me ("Antonia is a journalist, Antonia is an events planner") but that, at the same time, everything was desirable. Especially if it was others who did it, on whom everything seemed to shine.

I was looking for beauty. Better still, I was looking for a place for me in that beauty: to be a small cog in it. Someone capable of bringing it to others, of sending out smoke signals, of somehow saying, "Hey, wait, stop, look at this, if it's breathtaking to me, it can take your breath away too." But exactly how, I didn't know.

I fell in love with everything: the way a word sounded on a man's lips, the boy on the bus with a rose in his hand, embarrassed by the smug glances of us women. And I was amazed by the musician who transformed all these things into notes, by the photographer who could capture them. I read the books Vittorio published, chosen one by one—I knew that they would never disappoint me—and I could clearly see that he too had found a way to transmit beauty. And me? I thought and sighed when I returned home from a concert or the theater, or when I was just sitting on the floor, my back leaning against the couch, book in hand. What do I do?

Shortly after my date with Vittorio, I found a job in a small bookstore for children. Every morning, I had to raise the rolling shutter, dust the shelves, straighten the books, put them back in place. I swept the terracotta-tiled floor, turned on the computer, counted the money in the cash box, looked around. There was so much orange in that bookshop.

The first customers would arrive, the mail carriers came, the salesmen with their shoulder bags, the parcels of new books arrived, the packs of supplies. I shifted stacks of books, making them fall. With colored chalk I wrote down the day's story times, carried the small blackboard to the doorway of the shop.

Then I waited for the children. When they came, we sat on the floor and I began to read them a story.

Their mothers would say to me, "You're not from Milan, are you?" Then they vanished. "We'll be back to pick them up in an hour."

The kids didn't care where I was from or whether I read with a theatrical air or whether I had a shrill voice. We sat in a circle, I'd read with the book facing toward them as they gaped open-mouthed, rolled their eyes, and sprawled on the cushions, sucking lollipops and asking, "Why does the dragon want to eat the little boy?" The story continued. And bit by bit, they dragged their little bottoms to the center of the circle, closer to the book. "Move over, I can't see!" they squabbled. They would point to a picture. "She's a bad witch, see? Her fingernails are black!"

Then a little girl with thick, red-framed glasses asked, "Can I come sit in your lap?"

The others saw her rest her head on my chest as I went on reading; then they scrambled to their knees and looked at me, I pretended not to notice. Their eyes widened, asking permission. I smiled. And from that point on, I became a small mountain that they tried to climb, pressing round and clambering on my shoulders, my back, shouting, "Me, me!" until finally snuggling in the valley of my crossed legs, belly up and head down, all tangled up with one another. The story went on. Until we found ourselves completely stretched out, the open book over our heads like a roof and us underneath, laughing at it all.

I discovered that I liked it. That choosing the books to display in the window meant something. That talking about them could be exhilarating. That all I had to do was say, "I read this book" and describe it or just tell how much I had enjoyed it, and they, the customers, would buy it. "If you say so . . . ," they said, and I felt guilty because it seemed to me that I said the same thing about all the books I liked, that "so delightful" that always came to my lips, so visceral, not very professional.

They would come in and say to me, "I'm looking for a book that . . ." I'd search through the shelves. "Here it is!" and the book would be placed in their hands, with a description that they would listen to; at first, later on, no, later they simply trusted me. I had become a bridge.

At the end of the day, I put my jacket back on and slipped the books to be read that night into my bag. I checked the phone: no message from Vittorio. I turned off the lights, reminding myself to please not cause any problem when lowering the shutter. I'd jammed it three times.

Then Vittorio called.

"How are you?"

"Good."

My voice echoing in the phone, high-pitched, childish.

"Are you free tonight?"

Scratching my head, I tried to find a way to keep that voice from trembling.

"Actually, I have a birthday event at oTTo—is that its name? Apparently there's a concert, and a friend is celebrating there."

"Go on, my friends are going there too! There are the . . ." He said an English name that I didn't understand. Assuming it was English.

"Actually I don't know."

I was on the street, there was traffic, the screeching of a tram braking.

"I can't hear you well. Did you say something?"

"See you there," Vittorio decided.

We'd looked for each other in the crowd, in the dark nightclub. I had spotted him earlier, while he was with his friends, but he kept turning the other way: he was waiting for me. His curly graying hair, his broad nostrils.

"Don't go over," Gioia said. "Let him be the one to come to you."

Instead, "Vittorio." I tugged at his sleeve to make him turn around.

His face lit up.

We couldn't stop kissing. We didn't break apart for a second. Hands, lips, pelvis. He introduced his friends, a quick handshake in the dark, then we were back to it, locked closely. Kissing seemed so simple now. Offering my neck, running my hands over his arms to feel their form under his shirt. The concert, the birthday, there was nothing but his laugh, his lips on mine, his questions in my ear: "Do you have a boyfriend? How long have you been single? And how come?" My lies in his ears.

"You're not telling it to me straight," he said.

I didn't want to think about anything. Just for tonight, I told myself, just for tonight.

Vittorio held me close, gripping my hips. I was ashamed of that desire, of the boldness of his hands, of the boldness of my kisses, of his remarks—"What happened to your shyness?"—but I did nothing to put an end to it.

Then it was the evening that ended; Gioia came to ask me whether we would go home together.

"You're leaving already?" Vittorio asked.

"I guess . . . ," I said, looking at my watch and waiting for some sign that he would keep me there.

Instead, Vittorio took my hand, raised it to his lips, and made a brief bow, smiling at me.

"Who knows, maybe fate will let us meet again," he said.

Then he hurried to join his friends at the bar.

Reeling, I made my way shakily to the checkroom, where Gioia handed me my coat and scarf. The scarf fell, someone stepped on it; when I picked it up off the floor, it was filthy.

I turned around. I hadn't even gone out the door, and already Vittorio was laughing with the others, holding a large stein of beer.

The taxi raced through the all-but-deserted streets—three in the morning, someone at a bus stop stubbornly waiting for an all-night bus. I hugged my knees, chewed a fingernail, looked out the window.

"What's that skyscraper?" I asked Gioia.

"What now?" she asked in turn.

"Tomorrow I go back to normal life. Whatever happened tonight, tomorrow I'm going back to my life. It can be done, can't it?"

She stared straight ahead, a passing light illuminated the small round scar chicken pox had left on her forehead.

"It can," I repeated, without the question mark.

Gioia shrugged slightly, her lips turned down. "If you're able to, yes."

At home, I undressed in a trance, by the light of the table lamp. I gingerly took off the scarf with my fingertips. It stank of beer. I thought about the way Vittorio had held me close as we danced, about the pressure of his hands on my hips: "You're not so shy, then." I felt ashamed, a shame that seized my stomach. "I have to wash it," I said to myself, "or throw it out."

Instead, I put the scarf in a plastic bag and hid it in the back of the closet, like evidence from a crime scene.

That night Vittorio sent me a passage from a novel that felt like good-bye.

> *"The reason for constantly packing my bags, depriving any stay of meaning. Set sail, take off, from people from places from passions, a sad attitude in which to wrap up the few personal loves ever possessed along with old newspapers full of bad news. Why? You asked me. Who knows."*

A strange longing kept me awake, my head full of vague, drifting thoughts.

As dawn broke, I took the cell phone from under my pillow and gave in to a reply.

THE PERFECT ALMOND TREE
MIRRORS

The first time Silvia had seen Antonio, he was just a crazy airplane in the sky.

It was the feast of B.'s patron saint, and what Silvia would remember of that day was the heat on the crowded promenade, the balloon vendors, the swaying statue of San Nicola, and the expectant smell of liver sandwiches. She also would remember Miss Fortuna, head of the Association, who counted the panini every five minutes. "Let's not lose any." She laughed. And her fear when she realized that Dario was no longer holding her hand.

Then too, above all else, the *Frecce Tricolori*: the tricolored planes that did somersaults in the air, chased one another, crisscrossed, parted, regrouped, and when they were back in formation, flew even higher, leaving colored trails. "The colors of the Italian flag," Miss Fortuna had explained. Silvia had been entranced by the spectacle of zigzags and spirals, and Dario had teased her because she'd stood there gaping.

They had installed speakers on the seafront promenade, and an announcer's voice described the stunts, urging people to applaud, and sometimes saying, "Look to the right!" or "Look to the left!" And Silvia turned right, turned left, and the most thrilling moment was when the soloist reappeared in the empty, silent sky where only a few dissolving vapor trails remained, materializing suddenly from behind a building, just like that, and like a streak of lightning flying across the entire seafront, performing revolutions just a few yards above the water. "One, two, three, four, five snap rolls!" cried the unbelieving announcer, and everyone applauded loudly, hearts pounding, and Silvia most of all, because she wanted the pilot to hear and smile, upside down inside the cockpit.

At the end of the show, a child let go of his helium-filled balloon, and Silvia imagined it was a gift for the pilots; she hadn't taken her eyes off the sky until she and her companions moved to the auditorium in the town hall.

"Soon," Miss Fortuna explained, "the pilots of the *Frecce Tricolori* will be here and will tell you everything you want to know about their stunts. You don't know this"—she'd sat down next to Silvia—"but I've dreamed about meeting the aviators of the *Frecce Tricolori* ever since I was a child! It must be because I read Liala—have you read her? But what am I saying, you read Pessoa, Leopardi, Yeats! Do you have a poem for the feast today?"

Silvia always had a poem. Like some people always have a handkerchief in their pocket or a pen in their purse. Silvia always had some verse with her. But that afternoon in May, Miss Fortuna was asking her for a poem for the special day . . . Would she be able to find a poem to describe the occasion?

The aviators were lined up in front of them, in the municipal auditorium. They told their stories, described the years of training, the stunts that they performed earlier. They were all in uniform, tall and straight, sturdy. With the exception of one man.

He stood a step behind the others, he was not at attention and in fact was swaying slowly, shifting his weight from one leg to the other.

He did not have the proud look of a hero; rather, he seemed lost as he stared at them.

Antonio did not take his eyes off the young people with Down's assembled in front of him, thinking he had never seen so many of them all together. And the tingling in his chest grew as he wondered about their lives and what meaning it could have, ultimately why had God chosen that fate for some of his children? And why them and not him, for instance?

Silvia noticed that the aviator's face was beaded with sweat.

Were they aware of their affliction? Antonio wondered. And how great was their parents' anguish? Oh, he thought, if I knew that my child would be born with Down's, what would I do?

Look at that, Silvia said to herself, why is he touching his leg now?

Ouch, there, now my leg is throbbing, Antonio thought, I ache all over . . . Could I really have multiple sclerosis? I don't want to suffer, I'd rather die suddenly, anything but illness . . . Still, the doctor said I'm fine . . . True, but she didn't have them do an MRI . . .

Silvia's eyes popped when she noticed that the pilot, trying to avoid being seen by anyone, had slowly raised his right leg off the floor and was trying to keep his balance.

See that, Antonio? You can't keep your balance . . . It's all very well for them to say I'm a hypochondriac, I'd like to see them in my shoes. And why is that girl looking at me now? My eye, my eye is twitching . . . What was it I read? If it's the same side as the leg, it's a symptom . . . or is it the other side? Anyway, they've both gone into spasm. There, now I can't see anything . . .

What on earth is he doing? Silvia thought, curious. By now she was totally captured by that odd character and no longer gave a hoot about the others, standing there like mummies as they described their feats—because that guy was closing first one eye, and then the other, as if he were doing some tests, right there, in the midst of his intrepid companions, totally oblivious to the commander who was introducing the acrobatic squadron.

Silvia laughed delightedly as Antonio was now dripping with sweat.

"We present our team!" the commander said.

When it was Antonio's turn, Silvia couldn't believe her ears: that guy was the soloist? Come on! That was the hero she'd been cheering all afternoon?

However, when Antonio noticed that she was staring at him, a faint smile appeared on his face, which was white as a sheet; such a nice, open smile that Silvia changed her mind. All things considered, the soloist could only be him: among all the others, there was no one like him.

When they'd reboarded the bus that would take them back to San F., Silvia put her lips to Miss Fortuna's ear and whispered a poem:

> "There was a gentleman sitting in front of a lady sitting in front of him.
> To their right/left was a window, to their left/right was a door.
> There were no mirrors, yet in that room they were wholly mirrored."

"Beautiful."

12

I wrote about Silvia because I was lonely. Or was I lonely because I spent my time writing about Silvia?

One day I started to feel bitter. I'd made the apartment shine, bought drinks and snacks, polished my nails, and put on lipstick. Everything was flawless, including my Adelphi books in color order on the shelf, but I realized that it was all for no one. I knew the bitterness would not go away.

Life does not keep its promises.

I found no comfort in the streets downtown. I wondered where, in a city like Milan, you could bring that little bundle of sadness. Where could you stop and rest, if its streets were nothing but routes that led from A to B, as Vittorio said? Vittorio, who had disappeared, engulfed in his own good-bye.

I'd found myself in the gardens of the Gallery of Modern Art. Soon the lawn would flourish. For now, patches of snow melted among the tufts of grass. I thought back to Venice, about the nights spent talking about books. For Vittorio, it had to be run-of-the-mill, maybe even a headache, on some days. I might have had something to say, something to give to that world that gathered in the evening to dine in the finest restaurants, to talk about literature. "If only I had the chance," I told myself.

But there I was, sitting on the steps, the gallery closed, my hands freezing. I held them cupped under my warm breath, to no avail. If that was the only place where you could bring your sadness, it was cold.

Why didn't you do anything to make me stay the other night? I'd then texted Vittorio.

I didn't feel like pointlessly beating around the bush.

The response I'd received was one of surprise: *Why should I have? You wanted to leave.*

I gritted my teeth, caught by his logic. I picked up my purse to go.

Still, I do miss your lips. Another text had arrived.

I'm not just lips! I'd retorted angrily.

After that, the phone went silent for another ten days.

What I remember about Milan, about Milan as it seemed that night, I mean, are the open spaces—a portico, mellow lighting, muffled voices, and a river scent: no, it didn't seem like Milan.

"A river scent?" Vittorio asked. "Are you wearing different makeup? It looks good, you're beautiful."

"A girlfriend did my makeup. Just to experiment . . ."

Vittorio smiled at my confession, I got flustered.

"Yes, a river scent. I know there are no rivers. But it's as if I could smell a thousand canals beneath the ground . . ."

"There are the Navigli."

"Maybe it's just the scent of Venice that has stayed with me."

Vittorio laughed. Everyone knows that Venice stinks.

I said something stupid, I thought, why do I say stupid things?

"Well, for me that's how it is," I sulked.

He lit a cigarette and looked at me for a long time without speaking, wondering whether I was Alice in Wonderland or idiotic or whatever.

"I'm going to the ATM, be right back," he said instead. I stood alone on the sidewalk, my handbag dangling, watching stunning young women cross the piazza in short furs and high heels, looking like luminous trails in the darkness. No one seemed to notice. Milan is a city where no one turns to look at you.

But for the first time it was beautiful, that Milan with its bars under the porticoes, gas heaters lit, the muffled hum of voices, a gentle fog, and people drifting outside to smoke, wineglasses in hand. For the first time, while Vittorio was turned away at the other side of the piazza, putting his wallet back in his pants pocket, I felt as if my feet were planted in that piazza. I felt as if, from that moment on, Milan would make room for me too.

Even though those words about Venice's fragrance kept coming back to me—and Vittorio was not coming back—and I, looking at my shoes, waiting for him to return, wondered whether Milan wasn't simply a whore who has seen it all and therefore takes you in because she's used to doing so, not bothering to look at you.

Yet what I remember about Milan, Milan as she was that night, was my surprise at her cautious embrace. That and the river scent.

All through dinner I kept telling myself, He doesn't like me, I don't like him. Now he'll take me home and it will end there, and we'll both be in peace.

Vittorio ordered one glass of wine after another; I had a hard time finishing my fruit drink. In the end, he drank that too. I tried to tell him about my family, he replied that in his family it was just the opposite. I told him about a friend's comment: "She's concerned because she thinks I'm naive."

"You don't strike me that way." He shrugged it off with a note of finality as he sat there, rolling a cigarette.

I fell silent and he started talking again, offhandedly, *uninterestedly*, I kept telling myself with a certain relief (or maybe not).

"The bougainvilleas at my seaside home are growing too big. Next month I think I'll cut them," he told me.

"What? You prune your bougainvilleas in May?"

"No?"

I hid my face in my hands. "No, definitely not in the spring!"

"It's not that I'm pruning them because I think that's when it should be done, it's just that at this point they bother me; I stretch out in the hammock and the branches get in my eyes. And in any case, they obstruct the view of the sea."

"I can't believe it!"

"Why? Stop pulling my leg!"

We laughed. Sure, I thought, we could be friends. I managed to breathe.

Instead, as we were walking to the car so that we could each return to our own home, Vittorio stopped, drew me to his side, and kissed me on the lips; right after that, he went back to explaining how the Nobel Prize is awarded. I stayed behind, stopped at the kiss, he didn't notice. I hurried along, tottering on my heels, to catch up with him.

It was late, the nightlife had quieted down, only a few reminders were left, some beer bottles dumped under the Columns of San Lorenzo.

As I was getting into his car, he asked, "Do you want to come up?"

I stood there with the door open, struck—offended, maybe—by the predictability of the formula. Yet I sensed that in Milan, you didn't say no to Vittorio Solmani. Knowing that I wanted to, wanted to be with him, but that I shouldn't want to. And he was speaking to the part of me that wanted to say yes, and that was vaguely offensive: why wasn't I able to show him the other Antonia?

But there would still be the possibility, tomorrow, to retreat, to go back, I reassured myself, as he started the engine and fiddled with the stereo. As if nothing were irreversible.

He lived on the top floor of an elegant but shabby building with a large central courtyard. There was no elevator, so we climbed the stairs, him in front of me, two steps at a time, me one floor behind, on tiptoe so my heels wouldn't wake everyone, clutching the banister.

When we entered the apartment, he double-locked the door and did not turn on the light. He stood still in the dark foyer, as if he had suddenly lost his confidence.

"Want something to drink?" he asked.

"No."

For a moment he seemed bewildered. He turned on a lamp, took off his jacket. "Not even a glass of water?" There was a kind of pleading in his voice.

I shook my head.

"Maybe I'll give you a tour of the place . . ."

We stood there motionless.

Vittorio frowned; for a moment I felt a sense of satisfaction. Now, I thought, you'll have to get out of this yourself, Solmani.

He remained silent, however, ill at ease, looking at me with those big blue eyes that had forgotten the script.

He was wearing a dark blue sweater, his hair was disheveled. He was attractive, but it was an attraction that could still be resisted.

"Can I put down my handbag, maybe?" I came to his aid.

Then Vittorio remembered the lines that were expected of him, hung my bag on a coat hook, and came toward me in small steps. I heard my belly rumbling, nervousness. "Sorry," I said in a faint voice.

He put his hands on my hips and pushed me toward the bedroom, all the while kissing me. My body automatically obeyed.

Vittorio closed the door of the room with one foot; in the dark, I could barely make him out. He lowered the zipper of my dress, slowly. I felt my back exposed, my body losing its protection.

He gently pushed me onto a bed that seemed enormous. I thought that I had never made love with a man other than my boyfriend. Then I stopped thinking.

He crouched at my feet to slip off my shoes, fumbled. "How do you get them off?" He laughed. I raised him up to unbutton his shirt, I too faltered; he tried to help me, the buttons never ended. "Damn, how many are there?" he said. We heard ourselves laugh.

"*Shhh*, my neighbor," he said, still laughing.

We made love.

He caressed me for a long time afterward, teasing me about my embarrassment.

"Are you really ashamed?"

"Stop it!" I scolded him.

He laughed.

We made love again. When I tried to move, he pinned me down. "I'll decide."

"You don't get it," I replied.

Then he lay on his back, and I, lying on top of him, let him brush my hair away from my face and say, "You're beautiful, you're beautiful, you're so beautiful," with some surprise.

"In the dark," I countered.

"Okay then, you're beautiful in the dark," he teased as he kept running his hands through my hair.

But suddenly he broke away, turned on the bedside lamp.

"Shall we go?" he asked. "Otherwise I'll fall asleep and never take you back home."

He got up and quickly started getting dressed. He grabbed my panty hose and dress and tossed them to me so that I would do the same, and I rushed to pick up my undies from the floor before his hands could reach them.

I remember the windowsill, where an ashtray full of cigarette butts had been placed. I stared at it for who knows how long as Vittorio buttoned his shirt, put on his shoes, talked about the dentist appointment that awaited him the next day, and asked me for the thousandth time, "How old are you anyway?"

I forced myself not to look at anything else until I'd managed to assume a nonchalant expression. Like someone used to this sort of thing. On the windowsill the wind scattered the ashes of Vittorio's cigarettes.

In the car we didn't utter a word, the red lights seemed interminable to me.

At my house—on the corner actually, this time he did not accompany me to the door—Vittorio spoke, his eyes fixed on the steering wheel: "I don't know what to say, I'm sorry."

A fine drizzle beat a tattoo on the windshield.

I let a few seconds go by without speaking.

"Well then, *ciao*," I replied, holding on to my pride.

Getting out of the car, I dropped the book he had given me into a puddle. I picked it up, looked over at him as he sat rigidly in the driver's seat. I shrugged slightly as if to say, "No big deal, it happens." I don't know whether I meant the book or us.

13

Oh, it was such a sun-filled morning! I strolled along the Navigli and wandered through the flea market, its music in my ears.

I was enchanted by the antique desks and vintage tiled stoves, the typewriters and trays and silver spoons lined up side by side with their exotic shapes.

The wind made the stands' awnings flap, lifted the corner of a late nineteenth-century postcard. A vibrato of bicycles zigzagged among the crowd, amid the steady chatter—a gentle buzz—then turned onto the bridge and sped away, in pursuit of the first morning of spring.

The sky was blue, crystal clear, so much so that when a shadow fell over us, we all looked up in surprise; and finding a solitary little cloud, we were relieved that it was only a few seconds' irritant.

At the flea market on the Navigli, I realized that there was no reason to despair if I could not have this or that, if that gramophone would never be in my room. I had eyes to devour the beauty of those objects and an imagination that, in an instant, could place them in a house by the sea, the paint corroded by sea salt, or on a balcony in Rome, under a cascade of yellow hibiscus.

I might lack a lot of things, but an imaginary little room with an antique desk was mine alone and forever mine.

So I strolled around, feeling happy, happy to be there. Even though a few nights before I had wanted to die, and had told myself, Hang in there, you just have to hang on. I was right.

Sometimes, in spite of everything, life opens up, it concedes. And even if it lasts only an hour or two, it lasts long enough to remind us that no, we should not die when we feel like dying.

Maybe something of that sudden buoyancy had come over Vittorio as well because, although he had let many days of silence go by since our night together, he texted me as I was on my way home: *Shall we go together? I feel like ambling through the capital with you.*

The meeting to agree on plans was fast, almost unbelievable.

I got to the bar before him, wearing a white flowered dress and spring makeup. Vittorio arrived on a bike, a green Bianchi, which he carefully chained to a pole as I watched him from the entrance to the bar. He too stopped to look at me from a distance. He waved a hand. "Come on," and while I was crossing the street, he leaned his back against the pole, crossed his arms over his chest, and started giving me the once-over, enjoying the scene as I awkwardly made my way over to him.

"You're such an idiot!" I said when I reached him.

"And you're beautiful!" he said, and kissed me right on the lips, as if by now he had acquired the right to them.

In the bar, he opened the backpack he had over his shoulder and gave me some more books; he ordered coffee and orange juice, I a gelato.

"I'll get to Rome a few days earlier for some business meetings," he explained. "Then you let me know the day and time of your train, and I'll try to come and pick you up at the station."

"Oh. But where will we stay?"

"Don't worry about it."

He gulped down the coffee and disappeared within five minutes, climbing back onto the saddle like a cowboy.

There was still a week before our departure. Obviously, I wouldn't hear from him.

14

"'Reginella' is one of the most beautiful love songs ever written," Gioia says on the phone.

I call and ask her what the weather is like in Milan.

She lets me hear the music she's listening to.

"Do you go to the Galleria gardens once in a while?" I press her.

Gioia doesn't go there. She can't tell me whether the refreshment stand Vittorio regularly goes to is still open, she knows nothing about the presentation of one of his books at the end of the month.

"But you frequently pass the metro stop for the publishing house."

"Yes, often enough."

"And you never just happen to run into . . ."

"Antonia . . . ," she reproaches me.

Then I think, I'll get on a plane and go. I'll go, elegant as ever, hair swept up, face tanned, so that everyone in the metro will have to turn and look at me. I'll go to his apartment and tell him that . . . What will I tell him? That I accept everything, unconditionally? Maybe with a smile, so he won't find me too pathetic. All I want is for Vittorio to come down to meet me when I get there and ring the buzzer, and for a minute, just one minute, see his blue eyes widen with surprise.

Instead, "Gioia?" I ask my friend who is listening to "Reginella" at the other end of the line.

"Yeah?"

"What do you think people mean exactly when they say you'll get over it?"

Day Five: Add one cup of milk, one cup of flour, and a cup of sugar.

When I pour in the milk, the mixture seems to wake up from its lethargy: lumps float up, the mass swells. Even more revolting.

Nothing about this pastina-like mush that is left to rise would give you any indication of a cake. Only Anna looks at it confidently. She follows its progress day by day: in the morning she arrives at the house, sets down the bags with the shopping from the market, and observes the mixture with a clinical eye. She nods her head, satisfied.

"Is it normal for it to look like that?" I asked her today.

"Like what? It's coming along just fine."

Then it's time for the sugar and flour. The plastic cup, the same one from day one, is multipurpose. It's filled and emptied of sugar, measures the flour. That cup must feel proud.

Anyway, even if I'm not in Milan, I think as I refrain from mixing, I know exactly how he's walking now. With a spring in his step, sweater tied around his waist, legs wide apart, jeans slightly baggy at the knee. He'll stop by the newsstand, roll up the *Internazionale*, and stick it in his back pocket. Walking tall. He enters the usual bar and asks for a juice blend, vowing to buy himself a professional juice blender, he can already picture himself slicing up fruit on a Sunday morning (but he won't do it).

The mixture looks at me, its ugliness obscene. But also touching in its daily wait for some gesture from me. With the flour dusted over it in an attempt to cover it, it looks like the dilapidated roof of a shack.

"I wonder if he'll try to reject all this love?" I ask it. Then, at one point, the flour roof cracks.

From: antonia@libero.it
To: vittorioso@gmail.com
Subject: Suspected leak

Dear Vittorio,

What is time made of, drops? The drop of a first meeting, the drop of a step that leads us into a room, the drop of an afternoon of boredom.

The drop, a tiny droplet, of the moment that Sunday when you got up and left, slinging your backpack over your shoulder and disappearing on your bike, you blew me a hasty kiss; and I sat there numbed, eating my gelato, too big a cup, at the table in the bar, measuring the weight on the heart, how it shifts: now Vittorio is here, now Vittorio isn't here.

If so, I mean if time is truly made up of drops, Sunday's tiny droplet continues trickling relentlessly on my head. And there's no way to explain where the leak is coming from and how it is possible that the same drop of time does not die once it falls on my hair, but goes on dripping inexorably.

Antonia

THE PERFECT ALMOND TREE
THE HARVEST FEAST

The children slipped off while it was still dark, in single file. They slowly opened the doors of the houses, making creaking noises that their parents would pretend not to hear. For that night it was allowed. They made their way through San F., stumbling furtively in the hours before dawn, and as agreed, tapped at other children's windows. Then, in silence, more creaking, more unlaced shoes running after one another, more routes planned in a whisper. Hearts were pounding, "There could be dogs," hands were held and let go, "The night monsters may still be around," until they reached the fields and clambered up on the stone walls. Half-excited and half-contrite, their thoughts were with their mothers who would knock at their rooms and would not find them.

But the children felt big now, no matter if their feet didn't touch the ground and legs dangled from the wall. In the almond groves, the first morning light slowly filtered in. Already the stars could no longer be seen. The first birds began to sing. The children could feel their chests bursting with excitement. The early light advanced. And the almond trees, their outlines silhouetted in the dawn, seemed like profiles of women still asleep. The skeleton slender, but the flesh swollen, as women are in the morning, turgid in lassitude that slips away between the sheets.

The adults arrived in small groups; before the sun had completely risen, they were already in the groves. The men spread their nets out under the almond trees, and the women, sure of finding the children there, brought them a cup of zabaglione, since the day would require energy.

For each tree, a man climbed up to shake the branches from the top, while two others on the ground beat the boughs with sticks. Almonds poured down like rain.

It was a day of muffled sounds: the thumping of sticks; the small plops of almonds hitting the ground; the rustling of shaken foliage. Children chased one another through the trees, picked up the smaller sticks and played around, beating the trunks since they could not reach the foliage. Some of the adults lifted them up in their arms.

That day Silvia spent hours on the ground, on her hands and knees, gathering almonds that had fallen into and outside the nets. She competed with the others to see who could gather the most, and the numbers grew with their imaginings.

The women carried empty sacks, the youngest men filled them with almonds and lugged them to the houses. Finally, the men rested in the shade, wiping the sweat off their foreheads, handing around cold beers.

Now it was the women's turn. The children followed their mothers, cousins, and neighbors into the houses. Ten, twenty women of all ages sat around a large table. The younger children scrambled up on chairs, clutching the edge of the table to watch. The sacks were emptied onto the tabletop, and the women began husking the almonds, using stones and small fruit knives to remove the hulls. "Watch out for the lice," they said, and the children ran away screaming when clouds of aphids rose up. The women laughed and kept on working. The cloying smell of the husks filled the air, pervading the chatter about engagements and loves yet to come.

Occasionally a man would turn up, attracted by the female gathering, the ringing sounds of laughter, but he quickly retreated, driven off by the silence that greeted his arrival.

Meanwhile the women's hands worked tirelessly, turning black from the continuous shelling, smeared by the sticky sap of the greenest almonds.

Time flew by. The worktable became a sea of husks and shells, the almonds that had been hulled were thrown in the yard to dry in the sun, and the baskets with the shells were emptied: a torrent of shells, sharp clacking, like stones rolling around.

In the evening, when exhaustion was bone shattering and the children, wiped out by the games and excitement, gave in to sleep, the almonds were covered with a tarpaulin. The next morning they would again be left to dry in the sun. After that, the great almond harvest feast would be over.

I turned off the computer and peered at my blurry eyes in the mirror. Under what tree had I been born? Then I laughed at my nonsense, but I lowered all the shutters in the apartment—leaving Milan outside—stretched out on the floor, in the middle of the room, and the ceiling became a deep blue sky seen through the scattered foliage of almond trees. I no longer had a parquet floor under me, but clods of earth, and in my ears, Silvia's cries as she ran, chased by her cousin Eva, and whirled around the trunks, all excited; her wide skirts billowed as she ran, her bare feet sank into the soil; and at a certain point one of them shouted, "Race you to the sea! Race you to the sea!" And then I saw them sprint farther and farther away, sidelong, as my recumbent gaze permitted.

The cicadas remained, their unbroken singing, the branches of the almond trees already laden with fruit over my head, the bright sky beyond their tangled mesh—glimpses of San F.

Okay then, so the phone might not ring. *Ciao*, Vittorio, I'm sending you a postcard.

15

From: vittorioso@gmail.com
To: antonia@libero.it
Subject: Re: Suspected leak

I waited many drops before answering you. So many that you are already on your way to me, your train racing toward Termini, and if I don't leave the house right away, I'll end up making you wait on the platform. Track three, the station's website says. I hope to see you get off the train with wet hair.

I like your words. Tell me more, now that you're getting off that train.

V.

In Rome, you're caught. In Rome, everything beckons you, everything is a snare: the streets near Campo de' Fiori, which seem to go in circles, pursued by the fragrance of freshly baked bread; the many steps in the Monti district, brimful of promises; the light that turns languid in the afternoon, and, on the banks of the Tiber, flocks of crazed swallows flying from one treetop to another, peppering the sky with black. In Rome, you walk along weightlessly, and if your heart is heavy, all you have to do is go to the riverwalk, see Isola Tiberina embraced by the two arms of the Tiber, and the weight turns to dust—a pale, bluish dust that hovers just over the Tiber, and the next moment is gone. In Rome, a sorrow is a paper boat that is placed on the river and glides away.

The house had a certain Bohemian air: narrow stairs up to the second floor, paintings—unframed canvases—standing on the floor, wooden doors painted green. And a desk buried under papers and overflowing ashtrays.

"Whose house is this?"

"A friend's."

"A friend's?"

I still had my suitcase in hand. In the living room, Vittorio looked at me and laughed.

"She loaned it to me, she has another apartment in Rome."

"She's a painter?"

"Screenwriter. I had brought you something, but then I realized that I came here empty-handed, so I gave it to her."

"You gave her the gift that was for me?"

"Yeah . . ." He laughed, spreading his arms. "Come on in, put your things here."

The bedroom had pale blue walls. Simenon's *Blue Room*! I thought as I entered.

Vittorio leaned against the window, his legs crossed, and went on studying me. I was looking for a suitable place to set down my suitcase.

"When you walk into a room . . . ," he said.

"What?"

"You're so hesitant . . ."

"Hesitant? I don't know, maybe because it's not my house . . ."

"No." He closed the window, drew the curtains. "It's not that. I have a feeling I'll always see you enter that way, the way you walked into my apartment the other night, the way you're entering these rooms now . . . You're standing there asking yourself, Should I? Am I allowed? Maybe I'd better go?"

He put his hands on my hips. My breath caught.

"Why are you hiding your eyes? Look at me!" He laughed. "It's a good thing. I like it. I want to see you enter some more like that, on your high heels, so . . . uncertain . . . Swear to me that you'll always be bashful the way you're bashful right now!"

It was the first time we spent the night together. He held me close the whole time, reaching for me in his sleep whenever I moved away, grasping my ankle if I turned over.

Morning came and I hadn't slept a wink, I was so thrilled. It appeared as a light that seeped through the woven fabric of the curtain, barely stirred by the air coming through the window. A light that, as it crept into the room, became improbably blue. For hours I shifted my gaze from Vittorio's handsome face as he slept close to me, and the blue light filtering into the room.

That color of dawn in a room in Rome would remain the color of an unexpected joy that found me amazed and naked in the arms of a man I barely knew.

16

It was the first Sunday in May. There was a radiant sun, the first warm day of spring, and the climbing vines clung to the buildings along Via della Pace. Everything was asking us to slow down.

Instead, Vittorio was racing, his leather jacket tied around his waist, motorcycle boots on his feet, and that way of holding his head high that seemed to want to cleave the air.

I hobbled along. My high heels tottered on the *sampietrini* paving stones. I was wearing a beige cross-front duster, its fabric belt clasping my waist. The flaps swung from side to side to the breathless rhythm of my steps. Why the hell is he running? I fumed.

He'd stopped for just a moment at the newsstand.

"*La Repubblica, Il Sole 24 Ore,* and the *Corriere della Sera,* please. Antonia, do you want a paper?"

"No thanks."

"No?"

"I'll glance at yours," I replied faintly.

"Not even one of those women's magazines?"

The narrow streets around Campo de' Fiori had beautiful names: Vicolo dei Venti, Vicolo delle Grotte, Largo dei Librai—street of winds, of grottoes, of booksellers. On the streets there were artisan studios, cabinetmakers' shops, and a bicycle repair place.

I captured everything out of the corner of my eye while trying not to lose sight of Vittorio's shirt, which was already a distant spot blending among the tourists.

But a girl on a bicycle was enough to distract me: short hair, a beret on her head, and a joy in her eyes as she pedaled standing up. She disappeared with a loud ringing, her full white skirt catching the sunlight.

Vittorio turned and looked at me, disappointed. I hurried to catch up with him: Why doesn't he slow down, I thought, but my lips formed a smile to tell the women who were watching us, "Everything is just perfect, ladies." That morning I had spent half an hour putting my hair up in a kind of chignon—while Vittorio kept knocking on the bathroom door asking, "Are you ready?" and I struggled with the hairpins until one of them fell into the sink and got stuck—and now the strands were falling loose one after the other, so all I could do was hide my dismay and smile.

At the bar in Campo de' Fiori, he opened the paper and withdrew in silence. He took a bite of his croissant, felt about on the table looking for his orange juice without taking his eyes off the page. The man sitting next to us was watching us surreptitiously. I ate my toasted sandwich in small bites.

A few hours earlier, when I'd opened my eyes in our bed, the blue light had already retreated from the room. I got up to take a shower while Vittorio was still asleep, when his hand grabbed my hip. "Where are you going?" he said without even opening his eyes. I kissed his warm, full lips, exposed his even teeth, slightly yellowed from tobacco, and we made love without saying a word, eyes closed.

Then he opened his and they were like beacons: I felt something waver inside me.

It was then—he was lying on top of me, our bodies naked, for the first time I did not feel shy about mine—I took his head between my hands and said, "I'm . . ." Happy, I meant to say "happy." But Vittorio made a face . . . and the adjective that came out was "glad."

"I'm glad," I said. "I'm very glad."

"Ah. Good."

He'd leaped out of bed, picked up his boxers from the floor, and had not said another word to me.

Later on, at the bar in Campo de' Fiori, a father and a daughter sat down. They were French, and the little girl had a funny way of sucking up her frappé through a straw. She was wearing a red coat, a bow in her hair. She let her father know that she felt hot, her father crouched beside her and unbuttoned her coat, improvising a silly song.

Vittorio looked up, I thought he was about to speak, at last; I got ready to smile. Instead, he ordered a coffee from the waiter.

I started kicking the table leg.

"What?" He abruptly raised his face from the newspaper.

I pointed to the father and the little French girl. "Look how sweet."

"Hmm. If you want, take the section I've already read." He raised the newspaper in front of his face, so that only the boldface headlines were left for me to look at, along with the dismal gray newsprint, dirty, shoddy, resigned to being created for an hour more or less.

"I'm going to the restroom."

In the mirror I found my silk suit, the mole on my already tanned cleavage, the black eyeliner on my eyelids that accentuated my eyes. And I felt like a beautiful empty vase.

But then we started walking once more, Rome opened up, letting us look at her.

The ascent up the Aventine was bordered by rose beds, Vittorio's face lit up again. He talked, pointed out the views, I started telling him the names of the flowers and teased him about his obsession for knowing the names of things.

Vittorio quoted DeLillo, I listened to him, enthralled, wishing I could pick up every stone along that walk up the Aventine, one by one, to remember our stroll there.

Rome opened up, and a girl named Antonia saw the dome of Saint Peter's from the keyhole in the door to the Priory of the Knights of Malta and fell in love with Vittorio who, beside her, was taking pictures with his cell phone.

Then the sun started going down. On Via Margutta, the stone walls turned pink, the climbing vines gave way to a fragrant languor, and I felt like lying down beneath them. On Aventine Hill, the Orange Garden emptied out, the gate closed behind the man and the girl, they didn't stop walking and talking, a knot had loosened up.

From a belvedere, she pointed out all the places she'd like to see. She said, "Will we come back someday?" and awaited a kiss that never came. He tried to figure out the monuments, consulted an e-book guide without making heads or tails of it, then looked up and found her smiling ironically. "Are you making fun of me?" he said, then they started walking again, driven by a new exuberance.

In Trastevere, the walk livened up when they crossed the threshold of the neighborhood "bard," as the street performer called himself. With his thick eyeglasses and effeminate gestures, he was ready to declaim his poems to tourists sitting by the fountain in Piazza Santa Maria and in the outdoor cafés and trattorias—poems that made them laugh and listen quietly and that only he could recite, knowing the right pauses and sounds, the drawn-out way the word "acrimony" should be pronounced.

Tourists went on tossing coins in the fountains. The man was trying to find the way to the restaurant with his phone's GPS, walking with his eyes fixed on the screen, the girl tugged him gently by the arm when he was in danger of bumping into other people.

An actor wrapped in a long cloth coat hopped on the tram to go perform in a play about troubled marriages. He was trying to rehearse his lines, but he had *Orlando Furioso* in his head and he couldn't help it, he kept hearing the verses "That which a man sees, Love makes invisible to him, and Love makes the invisible visible." He looks like Pasolini, those who ran into him thought.

And so evening came.

At the Music Bridge, the dazzling white of the structure against the blue backdrop of the sky had something reassuring about it.

"It's spectacular," I said.

"Yet this too is contemporary art. Didn't you say that for you art stops in 1930?"

"I'm full of biases, okay. Do you have to point it out each and every time?"

"No, when you come right down to it, no."

We tried to reconstruct what was around us: the area above us had to be Monte Mario (did I see the lights of the planetarium?), farther on was Ponte Milvio, and what was that illuminated Madonna on the hillside?

"It should always be like this. Life, I mean, it should always be like this," I sighed.

"You don't ask for much!"

"You're saying we can't ask for a little happiness? Why can't we, tell me why. After all, it's not like we asked to come into the world."

Vittorio shook his head.

"It's no use stamping your feet. It doesn't work that way."

"It's just that the urge to be happy immediately, right now, is stronger than anything. Don't you feel that way?"

"Often it's the lure of happiness that makes us unhappy."

The incisiveness of that statement made me smile.

"So what should we do?" I asked.

"Acknowledge the naked truth of things. What is the happiness you're talking about, Antonia? The only happiness I know lies in not chasing after illusions, not telling oneself fairy tales. Being happy for our day-to-day struggle."

"Struggle against whom? And besides, what is happiness without illusions? What you say is awful. Anyway, for me the truth isn't enough."

"God," Vittorio said, rolling up his shirtsleeves, "it's incredible, you sound just like me a few years ago, the same way of tormenting yourself . . . Shall we go to Paris next weekend?"

I widened my eyes and didn't answer.

"My sister lives in Paris. You should meet her, she's fantastic. She's always been better than me at everything—even when we were kids, she was the studious one, accurate, intelligent. I, on the other hand, was troubled . . . a bit of a dickhead, to be honest! I lack the effortlessness with which she throws herself into relationships, the simplicity with which she's able to share her life with another person. For her it's so . . . easy, you know?"

He spoke those words as he rolled a cigarette.

I watched his fingers pile the tobacco on the paper and even it out with obsessive precision—he had such short nails.

"You're still troubled now."

Vittorio flicked his lighter a few times, shook it, then started slapping it against his thigh. Finally it caught.

"You're wrong. Hell, my friends envy me. They say, 'How do you do it? It's clear you're happy.'"

"You don't look so happy to me."

"Why do you say that? Why must there necessarily be some secret unhappiness?" A vein swelled on his forehead. "A person can be without hope and not be desperate," he spluttered earnestly.

I had nothing more to say and stared down at my shoes.

"Anyway," Vittorio concluded, "start making yourself happy. To believe that others can make you happy is foolish."

"We should be able to count on others."

"We should."

"And me, can I count on you?"

I gripped the railing of the bridge with both hands.

"How do you mean?"

"Can I count on you? If someday I might need . . ."

"No. Don't count on me, no," he said heatedly.

A long silence followed.

"What do you expect, Antonia?" he went on, more calmly, his eyes fixed on the wooden walkway, so like the deck of a ship. "What do you expect? Life is a desert."

Night had concealed everything, yet Rome did not cease being beautiful. That's how it is with Rome. Even if the monuments were not illuminated, even if Saint Peter's dome stopped gleaming under the starry sky, visible from every rooftop, even if Castel Sant'Angelo extinguished the streetlamps on its bridge and hid in the dark, even if the lights on the Janiculum disappeared, those on the hills, on a restaurant atop Monte Mario, even if all the lights on the ferries crossing the Tiber at the navigable part of the river were to go out, you would still hear her sing. A song to listen to sitting on the bank, legs dangling and eyes closed, while each second your heart seems to sigh, "I want to stay here, here, here."

17

Day Six.

Anna brought her granddaughter to the house and settled her in front of the TV to watch a cartoon show. I offer her some fruit juice, she looks at her grandmother and tells me, "I don't eat things that aren't made at home." Anna and I laugh; Anna says she doesn't know who taught her such things. She persuades her to accept the juice and a little later even a snack.

"Look, Antonia is making a cake."

The child slides down from her chair and comes to peek at my batter. I lower the bowl so it's at eye level for her. When she looks up, I am mortified. "It will look much better when we put it in the oven," I say defensively.

"Is there chocolate?"

"No, not in this one."

The little girl goes back and sits in front of the TV without commenting.

I'd like to explain to her that it isn't easy. Putting the ingredients together, keeping the memories under control, trying to . . . The point is that life doesn't for one second stop moving ahead: right now you're watching cartoons, laughing a little, maybe a bit bored, but at least it will be over soon; you'll put your Winnie the Pooh backpack on your shoulders and go home and eat things made in your own house, which you feel sure of. Whereas I will remain stuck in a Roman weekend, in the sweetness of memory, regardless of everything. In the bitterness of memory, despite the sweetness.

Meanwhile time passes, you know? One day without hearing from Vittorio, two days, a week, months. Before you know it, it will be years. And the lump in my throat that just won't go away.

I wonder if he's still spinning around like a top that won't be stopped. If he's found someone to merely watch him, enthralled, happy to abet him. If at the end of the day, in a moment of weakness, his eyes still seek arms in which to surrender. And I wonder if someone has already opened her arms to him. But then, even when they are opened to him, he never surrenders.

Whatever the case . . . *Day Six: Stir the mixture.*

Finally.

He would caress my knee. In the tram, while he was sitting and I stood in front of him and the passengers looked at us and we looked at them and, without saying a word, knew already what the other would say about each of them; in taxis, when the Eternal City said good night to us with its illuminated monuments and the sadness of departure was a sigh. He would caress my knee, and that seemly, delicate gesture restored me to love.

That was how Vittorio initiated me into his grammar of emotion, and I took pains to learn: It was up to me, to my womanly nature, to assume the burden of understanding. It was my job to decipher his language, to pave the way for him to find expression, an area in which he could extricate himself; it was my job, an almost religious duty, to compensate for the missing words, not with other words (which I dreamed of hearing, but no, they would not have been his), but with greater understanding.

We returned home, the last evening of our Roman weekend, and when I came out of the shower, I heard music that Vittorio had turned on—a poignant melody, but I couldn't make it out. I wrapped the towel around me and opened the bathroom door. From the doorway, I saw him in the semidarkness of the room, standing motionless at the window. He wasn't aware of my presence. The song lyrics went something like "save me, bring me peace." Vittorio murmured the words, his lips barely moving. "Don't leave me," he whispered. I felt my hand loosen its hold on the towel I had around my body.

It was then that it happened, like a sudden fit. Midway through the song, Vittorio fell silent, bolted to the stereo, and turned it off.

The next morning, he woke me, groping under my nightgown. He made love to me without a single kiss, not one caress. By himself. Then he turned his back to me and fell asleep again. I shook him, it was just a couple of hours until my departure.

"I can't take you to the station."

"Why not?"

"I have an appointment. We'll have breakfast, then I'll leave you at the bus stop."

In the courtyard of the café, children were playing around a small wooden house, their faces appearing and disappearing behind the windows.

"Listen, Vittorio . . ."

He turned on his phone and invited a friend of his to join us.

He had some flakes from the croissant in his beard. For spite I didn't tell him.

"Vittorio . . ." I tried again. "I'm . . . Well, I'm a bit confused."

"Confused? About what?" He stiffened.

"About this weekend."

"Why?"

"Because I liked being with you . . ."
"And that's a bad thing?"
"Yes, it is."
"Why?"
"Because I don't know if you liked it . . ."
There was a table between us.

Looking back now, it seems to me that we were always that way, Vittorio and I, always at a bar or in a restaurant, always restrained, facing each other across a table; with me acting as if nothing were wrong. I watched him read the newspapers, invite friends to join us, lean back in his chair, cool and collected, but deep down, I felt the urge to stand, hurl away the chair, overturn the table with the coffee cup, the freshly squeezed orange juice—his orders, always the same—to finally see those blue eyes widen with surprise, to sweep away that imperturbability, tablecloth, sugar packets, cell phone and all.

The fact is that I must have known, in some part of me, that two people who love each other don't spend their time sitting at a table in a café.

His phone rang.

"Hey! Fantastic, I'm here, I'll wait for you!"

He hung up.

"I honestly don't get it." There was irritation in his voice. "I liked being here, why shouldn't I have?"

He walked me to the bus stop. He kept looking at his watch and saying, "Where the hell is it?"

I was so humiliated, I couldn't speak.

Then the bus appeared at the end of the street, and Vittorio tried to take the suitcase out of my hands to help me carry it on.

"No!" I twisted free, angry.

He took my face in his hands and gave me a long kiss on the lips. I squeezed my eyes shut as tight as I could.

"I liked being here," he said slowly as the bus came to a stop, and I refused to look him in the eye. "I liked it."

Just before the door slid closed behind me, I felt Vittorio's hand on my shoulder, trying to hold me back. I left, aware of the utter sadness of that belated gesture.

THE PERFECT ALMOND TREE
BALANCING

Then Antonio actually ended up in San F. that summer. Silvia ran into him in the little square, while he was looking for the house of the cousin who was putting him up. She'd been crying on the church steps, for some reason that she no longer even remembered. She stopped him. "I've seen you before." And she showed him the way.

Ready to dash away, Antonio mumbled a thank-you, but she said, "Do you have five minutes?"

The smell of broiled meat drifted from a grill.

Antonio hesitated.

"Don't you feel well?" he asked.

"I'm a little sad, will you hold my hand?"

Antonio looked around and walked uncertainly to join Silvia on the steps. He gave her his hand the way one would offer it to the director of a bank. Silvia burst out laughing, her nose still running a little from crying.

"Why are you laughing?" Antonio asked, beginning to sweat.

"I like you, Mr. Aviator."

"Antonio."

"I know. I'm Silvia, if you like me. Are you here with your plane?"

Antonio stammered something about being granted a furlough. "No, a mandatory leave, to tell the truth and . . . well, uh . . . I'll be here awhile at my cousin's . . . No flying, later on, who knows, maybe they'll let me fly again."

"Okay. For now, remember not to get lost again! I'm going home. I've forgotten all about being sad." Before leaving, she turned around for a moment: "Anyway, if you ask me, you can balance on one leg only!"

The sky was clear, the square deserted. An orange Super Santos ball was wedged under a car, and Antonio suddenly felt better.

18

Vittorio did not bring me to Paris.

But in the months that followed the weekend in Rome, we did nothing but travel around Italy: the Amalfi Coast, Liguria, Versilia.

Vittorio liked to arrange to meet me in a different city each time. He went ahead, I joined him. We did not depart or return together.

"I like to meet in different places all the time!" he said when he saw me step off yet another train. He took my suitcase, gave me small, quick kisses. "Package picked up," he joked.

He noticed everything: "You're wearing your hair a different way?" "Is that a new dress? It's very chic!" He ran his hands through my hair, followed a zipper down my back, paused at my hips.

"How is it that you're more beautiful each time?"

And I, who all the way on the train had felt my legs trembling with excitement at seeing him again, remained frozen, speechless.

Often he welcomed me with absurd suggestions: "Shall we tour the city?" even though it was one in the morning and I was exhausted from the trip.

We left the suitcase in the car and walked through unfamiliar streets; he knocked at the already half-lowered shutters of bars to ask for a glass of wine, while I held back, embarrassed. "No, no, they're already mopping the floor, forget it." But Vittorio always got in; that infectious smile threw open all the doors.

He drank leaning against a wall, one hand in his pocket, his face more and more tanned, his hair frizzy from the sea air.

"A person who only drinks water is hiding a secret." He held his glass out to me to at least moisten my lips, his eyes mischievous.

He sang a tune.

"Do you know this song?"

"No."

"How can you not?"

He started singing it again from the beginning, complete with instrumental accompaniment: forehead wrinkled as he simulated a guitar solo, his expression concentrated, his voice hoarse.

"Recognize it?"

"No. But you're a true rocker," I teased.

"Really? I've always said so myself."

He drew me to him and sang in my ear, until his voice became a whisper, and meanwhile his hands circled my waist tightly.

I felt like a queen.

But all of a sudden a shadow fell over him. He didn't enjoy being with me. Not at all.

We were looking for the way back to the car, his eyes were glued to the phone's GPS, then he went on walking in the direction indicated, alone and silent. I felt the full weight of his disappointment. Who did he expect to get off the train? I wondered.

He drove with the music on; I rolled down the window and looked out, all the while hating myself for everything that I was not: lively, interesting, amusing, talkative . . . an endless list. Meanwhile I peered at myself in the rearview mirror, since by now my makeup had run and weariness made my eyes seem smaller.

But a few weekends later, there was another station, another city. And I rearranged my work schedule, canceled trips home, took pains to find train connections and the right handbags and shoes.

Everything was new, exhausting, and exhilarating.

We traveled day and night, on his motorcycle. As he waited on the bike and saw me come out the front door, his eyes widened. "You call those sports shoes?" "And where are we supposed to put this handbag?" "Take my jacket, you'll freeze to death with yours." Sometimes he sent me back upstairs to change, and all afternoon I remembered the face he'd made when he saw how I was dressed.

We slept in fabulous houses overlooking the sea, his or those of his friends, with the sound of the waves' lapping coming through the window; but sometimes Vittorio changed his plans at the last minute, and we found ourselves sharing single beds in one-star hotels.

We talked about happiness again and spent hours sitting on the floor, with the music playing and our eyes closed, telling each other what we imagined.

I watched him correcting proofs at a table on a terrace. His green pen scrawled indecipherable marks on loose sheets of paper.

"This character should speak in the first person," he said aloud. "No, here the author should be more bold."

"How do you do it?" I asked.

"Do what?"

"Read a story without getting into it."

"It's my job," he replied.

I made tea, quietly set the cup on the table, and started to move away. He pulled me by the arm.

"Thanks. What are you doing over there?"

"I'm writing."

So I stayed in the living room writing, with him on the terrace correcting proofs. When I looked up from my papers, I saw him through the window, his back bent over the pages, concentrating, his left hand closed around the cup of tea that I had made for him.

Everything was as it should be.

At sunset, we went down to the sea. "During the day, there's too much of a racket," he'd decided.

He dove in without waiting for me and took long swims, with vigorous strokes. I floated on the surface of the water, I let the current carry me away, and I felt like I was giving continuous thanks: to God, to chance, to Vittorio, to life, to whoever had brought me there.

The red of the sky was beginning to fade, the other swimmers were departing. We stretched out on a rock and lay there silently, wrapped up in our towels, two dark spots in an expanse of cobalt, until the last light of day disappeared.

"Thank you." I once let the words slip out.

He gave me a withering look. "I just don't get it when you do that," he replied sharply.

In the evening there was always dinner with some of Vittorio's friends: the best fish restaurants, bottles of wine that kept coming, arguments about the laws regulating book prices. And at the end of the evening, a joint was passed around from hand to hand, on a rooftop we'd climbed to for stargazing.

They didn't offer it to me, maybe because it's written all over my face that I'm not the type to smoke joints, or maybe because I listened to them silently the whole time, so it was easy to forget I was there. Vittorio was the first to forget me on those evenings with the others.

Then the weekend was over, I loaded my suitcase in the trunk of Vittorio's car, and we left for the station. In the car, he didn't say a word, and I began to wonder how many days he'd disappear for this time. The prescribed five? Ten, given that there was a book fair abroad? I slapped my hands on my knees, opened and closed my handbag, sighed loudly.

When would we see each other again if he had a wedding the following Sunday and a thousand other plans already made for the weekends after that? Had he liked being with me? Then why hadn't he kissed me since the night before?

Say something, Vittorio, I thought. Say some fucking thing.

And he said, "There's traffic."

He dropped me at the station and I ran to search for the platform.

As the train pulled out, I had the feeling that Vittorio had turned on the CD player in the car and started singing.

19

From: antonia@libero.it
To: vittorioso@gmail.com
Subject: Bougainvilleas in Otranto

Dear Vittorio,

It's four twenty on a Saturday afternoon. If everything is as it should be there, you will receive this message between the gratification of your four o'clock coffee and a sense of guilt (not very likely) over your four-thirty cigarette.

Hey, I see you laughing . . .

How is your "saunter" on the Côte d'Azur going? Did you don a straw hat? Noblesse oblige . . .

I am here at my family's. I let them prepare breakfast and dinner, make the bed, slip a sandwich into my beach bag. In a word, I'm being a daughter.

And I wonder what's become of a certain gentleman I know who dreams of hanging on to the steps of a moving train, a sleeping bag on his back, like Indiana Jones . . . Do you know him too? He has a grizzled beard, with a few nostalgic reddish hairs. If you pass by his house, it's likely you'll spot him on the balcony, pruning the bougainvilleas . . . That's right, now, when they're in full bloom!

"Well, the branches are reaching the hammock, they bother me!" he'd tell you if you dared offer some objection. Although I doubt he would speak about such a personal matter . . . He's very careful about certain things. About not opening up. I'm afraid that in the end he's come to believe that he is, in effect, able to hide. The fact is that in reality his plan is full of holes. Don't tell him, though, if you run into him.

Instead, look at his beard: If he scratches it, he's nervous. And if he strokes it, tugging the strands down one by one to the point, well, then you can bet that he wants to say something but is holding back.

He too has his moments of hesitation. An uncertainty, maybe. A temptation. To offer a caress, to say an extra word. But he tugs at his beard, and then you're sure he won't say it. You have to hand it to him, he has a certain discipline.

Still, it's nice to watch him skate through his life: see, he's the kind who is delighted that summer is approaching, that Marco Pesatori's horoscope comes out on Friday, that there's a bar where you can get a fresh-squeezed juice and read the newspaper. He has a gift for it.

In short, if by chance you see him, tell him that the girl who was in his bed—the one he thought was sleeping when he crouched beside her and asked, "Are you asleep?" kissed her lightly on the arm, then kissed her again, and again and again, laughing gently, until she stirred a little, and then he stood up and went into the other room—well, tell him that the girl wasn't really completely asleep . . .

But, well, she isn't like other people who accuse him of not being able to stay put. You have to make that clear to him. She doesn't think it's easy being the one who chooses to go into the other room. Tell him that seriously. And then change the subject.

Tell him about Signora Olga's fresh tortellini, maybe. And watch out! He steals them from your plate.

Antonia

I went home for a couple of weeks. I went down to the South, while Vittorio boarded a plane bound for France.

We said good-bye at his place, satisfied after a night together; we said, "Have a good time," "You too," and I imagined us as two tiny dots, which parted to go in opposite directions, but that would soon, inevitably, return to the starting point.

So my joy was complete when I left, with a kind of firm conviction. "Because by now we're close," I wrote in my journal. "There's no getting out, we're close now."

At home they found me different, more sophisticated, more mature, more . . . glowing? They couldn't say exactly.

"Maybe it's the new clothes . . . all those silk pants, all that beige . . . Did you throw away the colorful little dresses you had? They were so pretty."

"No, it's that short, short haircut she got."

"It's not that either . . . It's something in her eyes that's changed."

I let them study me and I smiled, then I grabbed my purse and went out to join someone or other, or even just to take a walk by myself around that city that was mine yet no longer mine.

I went around like someone who has a secret. I went to the beach, I swam for hours.

"Since when do you swim so much?"

"Hmm." I laughed. I thought that when I came out of the water, I would write to Vittorio, telling him how far I had swum and about those rocks in the sea where it was said that . . .

Meanwhile I dove in and listened to the sounds underwater, that muffled, soothing, elusive *bl bl bl*.

My mother came down to the lowest rocks to dip her feet in and watched me from the shore. I swam over to her and told her about him.

"We even went to a café where Pasolini used to go, great ambiance, very crowded . . . and at some tables you could see people writing in notebooks, or foreigners of various nationalities—not tourists, but artists—and here and there from the conversations, you knew they were planning exhibitions or concerts or things like that . . ."

She sat on a flat rock and listened to me.

"And him, what is he like?" she asked me one morning.

I was floating with my face upturned to the sun.

"A tormented soul convinced that he's happy! But when he speaks, you stand there with your mouth open . . . the things he says, the way he thinks . . . and then we talk about happiness—have you ever talked to anyone about happiness? I hadn't, not with anybody . . . And if you could see him in a crowd, how he loves talking with people, how curious he is about everything, how it only takes him a minute to understand someone . . . I feel like I have everything to learn from him. Above all I'm learning to measure my words, not throw them around so easily, to give weight to things that are said. He tones down my impulsiveness a little!"

"But are you happy?"

"Yes." I clambered onto a rock to get out of the water.

"Come out over here. From here it's easy, even I can do it."

"I did it. I have to get in shape. Vittorio takes me swimming in absurd places, you almost need a rope to climb down to the water!"

I peeled off my swim shoes, felt the scorching rock under my feet.

"Though at times he's difficult. He hates the phone, so we talk every four or five days, sometimes not for a week . . . I'd like to call him, tell him about my day or just about something I saw, silly things like that, but he's rigorous; if you shorten the times, he doesn't answer, it's as if he wanted to reestablish a distance."

Some kids came by on a pedal boat, their shouting filled the torpid July air.

I breathed deeply.

"But I have faith. I have complete faith in him, in the person he is. It's something that I feel coming from inside, a certainty, you know what I mean? In comparison, the walls he puts up are nothing. And then too, I'm stubborn, you know."

"Don't I know it! But stubborn people can be hurt badly."

I shrugged. "We'll see," I said. I wiped my hands on the towel and pulled a photo of Vittorio out of my wallet.

"Isn't he the most gorgeous thing you've ever seen?" I said, handing it to my mother.

Vittorio had been caught by surprise at his desk in the publishing house, wearing a stylish jacket, the pen in his hand raised in midair; it was a three-quarters shot, and he seemed to be talking to someone who was there on the left. His glasses did not hide the blue of his irises, and tiny sparks lit up his eyes: he was talking about his work, certainly.

"He's a handsome boy. Man, I should say."

"But this photo is at least three years old, I found it on the Internet. I don't have any of us: taking photos is too much like what engaged people do, according to him!"

I stretched out in the sun, out of breath. My mother came over to my beach towel.

"But why, if I may ask, aren't you two together?"

Her body cast a great shadow over mine.

THE PERFECT ALMOND TREE
FOR HIS NAME

"I'd like a new poem, please, Mr. Amilcare."

"Has something happened, Silvietta? Here, come in."

Old Amilcare preceded her with shuffling steps and stopped in front of the bookcase, running a finger over the book covers, in search of inspiration.

"Yesterday I saw a man again . . . He's not handsome, but he's funny, and I was crying, but when he came near me, I laughed and my sadness, well, I forgot about it."

"Ah!" Mr. Amilcare turned around. "Well then, you know what, Silvia? For today, no poetry. Tea is better, come into the kitchen. Tomorrow, when you've settled down, we'll read something together."

"Why not today, Mr. Amilcare?"

"My child, poetry is explosive! Best to calm down a bit before handling it!"

Old Amilcare had started reading before he could see over the table, and the only books in his house were his father's: works of Russian novelists and hermetic poets. He could only understand a third of what he read. However, when he closed the book, something lingered in his chest, suspended, a melancholy pleasure that floated right there, close to the heart. It was a painful pleasure, to tell the truth, and for a long time after he read, he remained dazed.

"I grew impatient with the chattering at home," he told Silvia, "so I went outside. I carried within me the fire that the book had lit and that I could not put out. Maybe it was a little of the main character's pain, a little of the narrator's anxiety, the kind that certain authors leave between the lines, and a lot of my emotions that clashed with the feelings that were recounted . . . or maybe they were just reflected; I think that was the point, they were reflected . . . Oh, but I wasn't cured of them in any way. And you, Silvia," he concluded, adjusting his glasses on his nose, "you may have almond-shaped eyes, but I see how you finger the books, I see how your eyes widen at seeing the exact word. Because even though for you it is sound, only sound . . . you sense that it is the right sound. It's precisely the right one."

Summer had exploded. A new light reverberated off the white Mediterranean houses, so similar to cubes; it assaulted the eyes, invaded the narrow streets, came through the windows. The sea seemed as happy as a child when his father returns from a trip, laden with gifts. The rocks glistened, the palm trees along the waterfront promenade were freed from the restraints that had bound them during the winter.

And when Silvia and her mother, Maria, came out of Mass in the evening, the lights of the fishing boats could be seen offshore.

Mother and daughter made their way home without speaking as old people dragged their chairs out to the street, in front of their doorways.

A quiet walk lay ahead, none of the frenzy of resort cafés, no restaurants with prix fixe tourist menus posted in large letters, no rides or stands, no bars with a water view. It was an old-fashioned town, good for strolling through. A town for buying fish on Sunday morning.

Night fell perfectly, with no smudges of red sunset. The countryside remained dark, the barking of dogs reminding you of its presence. Wrapped in the sheets, Silvia heard her cousin Eva open the gate that connected Silvia's house with that of her aunt, heard her climb the stairs leading to the terrace, just above her bedroom; heard her few, unhurried footsteps overhead. Then Eva sat down on the ground, her eyes turned to the sky, and she knew that Silvia would join her.

"Want to try one?"

Eva smoked contentedly, legs crossed.

"Cigarettes?"

"A cigarette!"

"No, no!" Silvia said, frightened.

Eva looked serene, counting the stars in the sky and the houses below them, never growing impatient if she lost count and had to start over. No hurry, she had all the nights in the world to smoke her Philip Morrises and count things. But while she gazed and slowly counted, she was actually planning her departure—planning it down to the smallest detail, because it would be an important trip. And she would not be coming back.

"Do you ever get scared by what you think?" Eva asked her one night.

"If I think bad things, I feel ashamed."

"And what do you do?"

"I don't think about them anymore. And if they're really bad, I slap my hand, but not always."

"Not always?" Eva laughed. "You shouldn't slap yourself. I have bad thoughts too, sometimes, thoughts that could hurt some people, if they knew . . ."

"What thoughts?"

"Different things . . ." Eva hedged. "I wish I too could slap myself and think about other things, like you do . . . but I can't." She lowered her eyes and began pinching her thigh. "I don't think thoughts should be obstructed, they're meant to run, to fly far away, where your legs can't carry you. I think my thoughts can replace what life won't give me."

Silvia did not grasp the import of what Eva said, but she drank in the sound of it, enthralled, and felt that those words, however obscure their meaning, also applied to her.

The sheets hung out on the terrace billowed and sagged with the wind.

"But I won't lead you down the wrong path—" Eva broke off.

"I like your wrong path!"

They laughed.

"'Path' is a beautiful word," said Eva, suddenly very serious. "It has a beautiful sound. It hints at . . . freedom . . . I don't know, it's beautiful."

"That's true, it's beautiful."

"I like 'prospect' too, and you . . . do you have a beautiful word? A word whose sound you love, which you'd repeat a thousand times?"

"Antonio."

And she said it so candidly, so naturally, that no name was ever uttered with such love, and for a moment the world seemed to tremble under the caress that was Antonio's name pronounced by Silvia.

20

From: vittorioso@gmail.com
To: antonia@libero.it
Subject: Never lower your guard (bougainvilleas in Saint-Paul-de-Vence)

I've met him, that poor devil. No doubt about it, an apt description.

Never underestimate a girl who sits silently reading a collection of poetry: she seems harmless, yet there she is behind the book, studying you, analyzing you (how do you do it, do you take notes too?) and, quiet as a mouse, she gets to the most intimate part of you.

But then, I don't know about you, but to me that guy is somewhat likeable, after all . . .

V.

You may capture a part of a person that he himself is unaware of, but that doesn't make you welcome in his life. You may realize that it is only through your love for that man that you are able to reach the most hidden part of yourself, and ask nothing more than that fulfillment, frightening and astounding, that has little to do with happiness, because it is in fact greater than happiness, whereas for him you are instead . . . flesh, nothing more than flesh to caress. Not that there is any malice in that: it's just that each of us demands what he wants.

Elated by Vittorio's e-mail, I invited him to join me for a couple of days. I sent him a photo of my tanned body. Vittorio didn't even answer.

The guidebook for Apulia was left at home, underlined, full of Post-its and imagined outings, and I went back to Milan. Back to nights with the TV turned on, muted, and the clock ticking on the wall.

"We two, what are we?"

I had chewed over that question for hours before being able to spit it out. It was there on the tip of my tongue, but as soon as my lips parted, my voice failed. My nerve failed.

God, I thought, why am I afraid of this man? It was his cold eyes that petrified me, but above all his voice, which never cracked.

Vittorio was smoking at the window, serene and absent. He whirled around. "What does 'we two, what are we?' mean?"

From the apartment below came the rhythmic blows of a hammer. I was still in bed, wearing a T-shirt.

"What are we?" I repeated.

"You need definitions?"

There she is, already backed into a corner, the predictable, conventional girl who needs to tell her friends she's engaged.

"I don't need definitions. I need to know."

"What do you want to know?"

"Vittorio, I can't stand ambiguity." I tried to recite the speech I'd rehearsed a thousand times in my head. "Anything but not ambiguity. I have no idea what you think of me . . . You—you never speak, you come, you go, you never say a word, I—I don't even know . . ."

"You want to know if I see other women?"

My hand stopped wrestling with the folds of the sheet.

"Why, do you see other women?"

"No. But I don't think, at least given the way things currently stand with us, that I have to explain myself for that. But no, I don't see anyone else, I don't feel the need."

"Oh."

"Okay?"

"Okay . . ."

He came and sat on the bed, put his hand on my knee.

"Maybe I should talk more?" he asked. But there was no sweetness in his voice.

"You don't have to, but you would make things easier for me. I'm not asking you to be accountable to me for your life, I'm asking you to at least let me know what you think of me."

He lit another cigarette.

"Vittorio, you're hopeless!" I buried my head under the pillow.

"I'm hopeless?"

"Yes, you are. How can you not say a word?"

"Antonia, I can't." He sprang up. "It's hard for me. There are words I just can't say."

He started pacing around the room, inhaling the cigarette smoke, then tapping the ashes on the windowsill, beside himself. And there I was, my head half-buried in the pillow. I pulled it over my face completely and closed my eyes.

Long minutes went by. Then I felt Vittorio's weight on the mattress next to me.

"But, if you must know, I think you're really you, you're perfect."

"But I'm not really me," I said slowly, with profound sadness.

"No?" He lifted the pillow under which I had retreated. I did not look at him.

"No. There are a thousand things I want to tell you, a thousand things I want to ask you or do, but I hold back. With you I always have to restrain myself, bite my tongue."

"Really? I find it funny that you want to tell me a bunch of things and then you keep it in! So you're actually a pain in the ass?"

He made me laugh. I managed to look up at him.

"Yes, I am."

Vittorio moved the pillow off my face.

"It's just that today I really couldn't keep quiet any longer and . . ."

"Look, Antonia, if it makes you feel better," he said seriously, "there's not much to say or know."

He rested his forehead on mine. I felt the warmth of his skin, his nose brushing mine.

"I think I like talking with you. I like making love with you. I like the hours we spend together. When we see each other, I'm happy. What more do you need?"

The room seemed to tremble beneath me.

"I'm so silly. Stop, don't say anything more, it's enough."

I embraced him. His body remained rigid, but I didn't want to acknowledge it.

"Are we done with the interrogation for today?"

"Yes, you can breathe now! How many cigarettes did my first serious talk make you smoke?"

"Too many. Don't ever do that again!"

We laughed. I reached for him again, but he slipped away.

"I'm going to take a shower."

21

I entered the bookshop, and there was that orange awaiting me. And soap bubbles drawn on the walls with a quote by Munari. It was hot in Milan, the children were mostly all gone, now only a pair of twins came to hear me read.

Still, there was a joy in there that I could not have explained.

So when the owner asked me whether I would like to continue working in a bookstore, I said yes. It was when he asked me, "What if I told you that I'm opening a shop in your area that needs its own staff?" that I was nonplussed.

Vittorio came to pick me up at work that evening. And I skipped around him excitedly. He made a jealous scene. "Look at how your coworker is ogling you. Does he or doesn't he know that you're going home with me tonight?" he said, handing me the helmet.

"Here they can't keep me on once I'm done substituting," I told him. "When Fabiana returns, I'm out. But there may actually be an opportunity down where I'm from; he's opening a new bookstore . . . Can you picture me in a shop like that?"

"Of course."

"I might sell your books, can you imagine?"

"You'd be capable of selling my books even to me," he replied, kissing me.

We ran to make love that night. Afterward, as Vittorio slept on my belly and I stroked his hair, I envisioned selling his books. It would be like becoming an extension of him. "That's what I should do," I said to myself as he mumbled something in his sleep.

But I could not go home.

THE PERFECT ALMOND TREE
BARCAROLLE

Ruggero and Maria are dancing to Offenbach's "Barcarolle." It is evening and they have just finished dinner. They left the table without clearing it. Maria motioned, uncertainly, to say that they should first put the dishes in the sink, at least. But Ruggero took her hand, bowing slightly, and led her into the living room; the recording was slightly scratchy.

The music filled the room. Silvia got up from the table, on tiptoe, and stood in the doorway, watching her parents dance, only a faint beam of light from the kitchen.

Now she sees it, the music drifting through the living room, the notes creeping under the carpet; like a gentle stream of water they course everywhere, under the table, around the chairs; they climb up the walls, they settle on the silverware.

Silvia goes over to the window. The music swells, she rests her forehead on the glass. Her breath fogs it up. When the vapor dissolves, the reflection of Maria and Ruggero appears, their slow circling, their being happy at times, but almost in an undertone.

Silvia would like to stop time. This is her home. This is her family. Her parents are dancing after dinner. These are, perhaps, two people who love each other.

And she can almost picture herself, with Antonio, dancing in that same room: she clinging to his tall shoulders, and awkwardly stepping on his feet.

But at this thought, something inside her falters: the music is too beautiful, the happiness too great to even be imagined. The last notes fade away in the living room.

22

It was Vittorio's birthday. He already had dinner plans, but I said, "I'll wait for you." Gioia invited me to spend the evening at her apartment. I arrived carrying the dress for the occasion on a hanger.

"Wow, really!" she teased, taking the ice cream that I had brought.

We cooked a plate of spaghetti, singing "Let's Spend the Night Together" by the Rolling Stones, then I went into the bathroom to change and Gioia turned on the TV.

"Black or blue?" I shouted from the bathroom.

"What?"

"Eye shadow!"

At ten thirty I was ready. I sat next to Gioia on the sofa, in front of a ridiculous program, raised the sound on the phone up as high as it would go.

"What time is he coming anyway?"

"I don't know how long the dinner will last."

"But who is he celebrating with?"

"I don't know, the family, I think he said."

On the table, the remains of the ice cream melted.

"Was that a yawn?" Gioia asked.

"No, no."

"Liar. May I remind you that you've been singing 'Let's Spend the Night Together'!"

I responded by pinching her arm, and stretched my legs out on the coffee table.

"Why don't you send him a message?"

"No, I don't want to pester him."

"Okay." Gioia sighed. "But take off your dress, it's getting crumpled."

We rested our heads together and fell asleep.

Vittorio phoned after midnight.

"I'm done, I'm coming to abduct you!"

I leaped off the couch and stumbled over Gioia's shoes. I gave her a kiss as she slept, and I crept out.

I hadn't bought a gift for Vittorio, and he didn't offer me anything. But I had chosen the most beautiful dress I had, blue silk, and he made me twirl around in the middle of the sidewalk so he could look at me.

"You're ravishing."

I raised the dress all the way up to climb onto the motorcycle. He found it funny.

"I'll be the envy of all of Milan. I'm almost tempted to take the long way around!"

He drove to the publishing house.

"What are we doing here?"

He helped me unbuckle my helmet, ruffled my hair.

"A tour!"

"I've never been in a publishing house."

"All the more reason."

Vittorio locked and unlocked doors, pointed out offices and desks, opened cabinets full of books. He did not turn on the lights, so we went around by the sole glow of the streetlamps, which were at window height.

With a kind of apprehension, Vittorio watched me walk through. Maybe it was because of the cautious way I had of moving forward, as if I were entering a church dressed as a tourist; or because of the restrained tone in which I said "lovely," when what I wanted to say was "fantastic." He didn't take his eyes off me for a moment.

"This is my desk." He lit a small lamp. The computers were turned off, only one of them had its monitor on, in sleep mode.

"What is it?" I asked Vittorio as he stared at me.

"Nothing." He shrugged, and for a moment a tender expression crossed his face.

Only for a moment, in which I told myself, He loves me.

I took a couple of steps toward him, but my heels tapped on the floor and I felt self-conscious, I don't know why. Maybe because of my awkward body, because of the shoes that made noise, because I didn't know what to do with my arms now that Vittorio had opened the door a chink and I should have put my foot in it so as not to let that door close: it was the right moment. But a car horn blared in the street. Instinctively I glanced toward the window, and when I looked back at Vittorio, something had changed. He was searching for cigarettes, patting his pockets.

That night, his resistance was cracking.

I rushed over to him, stopped his hand.

"What are you doing, smoking?"

He smiled. At my fretting, at the impulsiveness of my words. He gave up the tobacco.

"You don't know how wonderful it is that you're here."

He said it without touching me.

The lamp's lightbulb blinked on and off intermittently.

"Will it last?" I asked.

"I don't know."

He buried his face in my neck but did not kiss me.

I placed a hand on his back. I wasn't used to hugging him out of bed. He didn't move, but I didn't have the nerve to put my other hand there as well. We were walking a tightrope.

Vittorio turned away, went to open the window, lit a cigarette.

"Come here." We looked out together.

Milan, which had become recognizable, familiar.

The filmy yellow of the streetlamps poured over everything. The gates to the public gardens were closed. How much night there was in the dark green of the hedges.

"You're good for the most vulnerable part of me."

I looked at him, hiding what I felt. To play it down I said, "Does it exist?" I bit my lip.

"It exists." He laughed a little, somewhat bitterly. "But you read me inside. You make me see things about myself that I didn't even know were there, that I discover only when you put them into words. I don't know how you do it . . . How do you do it?"

I was a step away, just one step away from him. On the desk, the table lamp's light began to flicker. I didn't move a muscle, our battle was all in the eyes. Vittorio did not want to be swept away.

"Does it scare you?"

"Don't stop doing it," he replied peremptorily.

I reached out to take his hand, or maybe I only thought about doing it; that night, whole minutes went by between a desire and a gesture. During those minutes, Vittorio moved; he disappeared into the room's darkness.

He returned to the window with a book, he stood with his back to the streetlight, opened the book to a page he already knew. He cleared his throat, pretended to gargle like a consummate actor, we laughed. A gust of wind ruffled the pages.

> "If only I had met Molly sooner, when it was still possible to choose one road rather than another. Before

that bitch Musyne and that little turd Lola crimped my enthusiasm. But it was too late to start being young again . . . We grow old so quickly and, what's more, irremediably."

How serious Vittorio was, all of a sudden. Behind him, the tall, narrow window.

Milan asleep out there, I thought, what can you know about it? That while you sleep, a man is reading aloud to me in an office of a publishing house, and every so often his blue eyes look up from the page and plant themselves in mine, so that I no longer know what to say and nothing seems real to me; and yet it is real, and you, Milan, are asleep, and for you we are simply a lit window, a dark silhouette against the light, while I, a speechless girl, try to appear nonchalant and can't manage it, because such a thing has never happened to me.

> "I was afraid of hurting her. She was so easy to hurt . . . 'Believe me, Molly, I love you, I always will . . . as best I can . . . in my own way.' My own way didn't amount to much.
>
> "Then came the moment for departure.
>
> "'You're already far away, Ferdinand. You're doing exactly what you want, aren't you? That's the main thing. It's the only thing that counts . . .'
>
> "The train pulled in. I wasn't so sure of my plans once I saw the engine. I kissed Molly with all the spirit I had left . . . I was sad for once, really sad, for everybody, for myself, for her, for everybody.
>
> "Maybe that's what we look for all our lives, the worst possible grief, to make us truly ourselves before we die.

"Years have passed since I left her, years and more years . . .

"Good, admirable Molly, if ever she reads these lines in some place I never heard of, I want her to know that my feelings for her haven't changed, that I still love her and always will in my own way, that she can come here anytime she pleases and share my bread and furtive destiny.

"To leave her I certainly had to be mad, and in a cold, disgusting way. Still, I've kept my soul in one place up to now, and if death were to come and take me tomorrow, I'm sure I wouldn't be quite as cold, as ugly, as heavy as other men, and it's thanks to the kindness and the dream that Molly gave me during my few months in America."

Vittorio closed the book.

That night was a long, dizzying fall, the kind you find in the videos of the groups Vittorio liked, accompanied by the pounding of electronic music and, above all, by the high notes of a singer's voice.

23

I take a breath. It's not easy to tell this story. Every so often I have to stop, monitor the turmoil that an emerging detail triggers.

I go out on the balcony, I observe other people's lives, I look for elementary actions: a woman taking in her laundry before it starts to rain, a hand that hastens to lower the shutter. So something uncomplicated, something simple really does exist?

I too could put down this pen, pull on a sweater, brew some tea, and wait to get over it. Because I will get over it, sooner or later.

"But you want to hold on to the pain," a friend told me a few days ago.

He is a man much older than I am, we respect each other, we understand each other. But I'm not sure he's right.

Do we remember in order to cling to something that has passed or to save it from oblivion? They're not the same thing.

I took my jacket and left the house. I walked in a kind of daze: it seems the end of a love never ends.

I entered the workshop of an Argentine craftsman who makes hourglasses. An entire shop filled with hourglasses of all sizes, shelves and shelves of sand slipping away. The Argentine was listening to a CD from his country, a poignant melody.

I wandered among the shelves, I picked up an hourglass, turned it over. The sand flowed from one side to the other, then again from that side back to the first one, and I kept feeling a knife in my belly.

The craftsman threw me a look from the rear of the shop.

"Have you ever loved someone like that?" I wanted to ask him, "Like a prayer, I mean. Me, I loved Vittorio like a prayer. There was the same silence, the same meditation, the same devotion."

He looked down and went on polishing a piece of wood.

I bought it, that hourglass. The man wrapped it in some beige paper, then looked up. As I rummaged through my handbag for my wallet, he said, "It hurts so much to have a heart."

Today is no day for that cake. As if time no longer existed. It's the perpetual absence of Vittorio, the rib that is no longer in my chest.

THE PERFECT ALMOND TREE
THE FEEL OF LIGHT

Antonio would tell her about his most stunning flights, the ones at daybreak, and how everything was delicate and peaceful: the changing colors of the sky, the way they blurred and blended into a thousand nuances; the clouds beneath the plane, one moment blue, the next gray, and at some points already awash in orange, and those that sailed along, solitary, almost evanescent, and those that formed tenuous banks and slowly broke up, giving way to the first rays of the sun; the silence that permeated everything, so that even the engine seemed to whisper to its pilot, "Be quiet, Antonio, let's not breathe, let the day be born slowly."

Antonio, who smiled at her more than at first and who at times, however, looked away. Antonio and his white teeth, Antonio and his kindness in helping Maria carry chairs for the neighbors. Antonio and the empty glass he held for hours so he wouldn't seem rude by getting up to put it away while Ruggero spoke to him.

Antonio who would become captivated gazing at the sky and the planes that streaked across it, and who would suddenly touch his wrist to take his pulse; Silvia wanted to stroke his hand and tell him, "Don't worry, you're fine."

Antonio who took walks with Silvia, and saw her wander through town following the sandy footprints of beach sandals and find an excuse to veer off toward Mr. Zeno's refreshment stand; every day she had him teach her the name of a new flower, and she would repeat it along the way to bring it to her father as a gift, intact. "*Strelizia strelizia strelizia strelizia,*" "*centaurea centaurea centaurea centaurea.*" Antonio who learned to hold her hand every now and then.

Then Eva would join them with a beach towel over her shoulder, shouting, "That's enough! Let's go jump in the water." And so they did, obeying her immediately, because Eva was a goddess in her yellow shorts and colorful flip-flops.

Eva and Antonio sometimes went out in the evening, they'd go have a beer at the bar in town or go hear a band in some nearby club. Silvia stayed home. She eagerly awaited the following day so that Eva might tell her something, but her cousin was vague and most times couldn't be found. Those were days when Silvia couldn't do anything at the Association, she couldn't paint, couldn't dance, wouldn't play with the others. The only thing she felt like doing was listening to Miss Fortuna tell the story of her past love: she made her repeat it again and again, then sat with her head down on the table, and not even her friend Dario could make her look up.

Those were days when Ruggero and Maria paced around the house like caged animals. They suggested the three of them take a trip, to visit places they'd never seen, meet new people, but Silvia shook her head, stamped her feet, and ran off to see old Amilcare.

"Those of us who are born and raised here, we have the sun inside us," he told her. "Only sometimes the sun burns."

24

"Things don't exist if we don't know their names." It was he who'd said it, that day on the Aventine.

To us, Vittorio had not given a name.

"Thing." That's how he spoke about us. "This thing between us," he'd write. I replied, putting "thing" in quotes. He continued unfazed.

"There are people who wait for their children to grow up before giving them a name," Gioia said. I sought comfort in that thought. It seemed to me that there was poetry in it. Or something like an awareness that could only escape a girl like me, but that Vittorio must possess.

But without a name, we were nothing.

"I'm with Antonia," he would say, answering the phone. "This is Antonia," he introduced me when we ran into someone he knew at a restaurant.

Antonia who?

Without a name, I had no rights—to ask him the reason for his silences, why his phone was unreachable for days, or even to make breakfast for him.

"What is all this stuff?" he asked me one morning when I got up the nerve to do it. "Pastries? Cakes? You treat yourself well!"

"Actually, I made them for you . . ."

"Thanks, but I'd rather have breakfast at the bar. You eat them, take your time, I'm going."

I remember the blue of the tablecloth, I drowned in it for a long time.

It was the urge to vomit that roused me.

I jumped up, knocked over the stool I was sitting on, I was already in the hall when I heard the metallic thud on the kitchen tiles. I grabbed the knob, it was gold-plated, but I couldn't open the bathroom door and I slumped to the floor. Something pressed on my sternum—a hand? I kept retching.

I breathed in, but it was as if I couldn't get any air. Try again, Antonia, I told myself. Try again, all you have to do is breathe, just breathe. But I couldn't. I gasped like a fish out of water.

"Don't you have a doctor in Milan?"

"No."

"You'll have a long wait, then."

"All right."

Everyone in the waiting room of the ER was accompanied by someone. I had walked there, staggering, alone. I'd tried to call Vittorio, he hadn't answered, so I texted him. Gioia's phone was off, afterward I would remember that she was away.

A girl came in, her face covered with bruises, her fishnet stockings torn. Her hair was closely cropped in a crew cut, an orangey color that made you think of the good fairies in cartoons. She whispered with a doctor, he went away, leaving her sulking. I motioned to her that the seat next to me was free. She looked at me, frowned. She remained standing, proud. I swung my legs nervously. I too was afraid.

"Can you positively exclude the possibility of being pregnant?"

The doctor was filling out a case report, and after each question she gave me an accusing look. She tapped the desk with the pen cap if I took too long to respond.

"Positively, no . . ."

"Can you positively exclude having contracted a venereal disease?"

"No . . ."

"Are you engaged?"

Vittorio called as soon as he read my message.

"Let me know when they tell you something."

I was shuffled from one department to another. Every doctor claimed that it was not within his jurisdiction, saying, "You should talk to your doctor." I kept saying, "I'm not from Milan." "The doctor of a friend?" And he wrote the name of the next ward I should go to on a slip of paper.

I got lost several times, knocked on the wrong doors.

I waited to see Vittorio arrive.

He must be tied up with authors, but as soon as he's finished he'll come, I tried to convince myself. Maybe he's asking his colleagues to speed up the meeting. Now he must be gathering his things, issuing instructions for the afternoon. He's probably looking for a helmet for me—would the car be better? he's wondering—and anxiously searching through his jacket pockets, unable to find his keys.

Every time the waiting room door slid open, I sat up straight and pushed the hair off my forehead.

I made my way home exhausted, disheartened. It was getting dark, the shutters of the shops were being lowered.

I entered and left the pharmacy, I was just in time to buy a bag of candy at a grocery: it seemed appropriate.

Under the arcades there were only a few passersby besides me. So this was loneliness? Nothing dramatic, nothing spectacular. Rather a slow trickle, something to be ashamed of.

Things around me were now just things, nothing more. They no longer spoke to me. A column. A torn poster. A sign, "For Sale Please Contact . . ."

So is it hope then that transforms things, that lets us glimpse something more?

I sent Vittorio a text, I didn't feel like talking to him. I explained that the diagnosis was inconsequential, nothing to worry about. His reply was one word and an exclamation point: *Great!*

A bus passed that went to my house, I let it go by.

Imagine that, I said to myself, who would have thought something could hurt that much?

25

I'd stocked up on chocolate eggs and kept them on the bedside table: if I could make it through the day without giving in to the temptation to write to Vittorio, in the evening, before falling asleep, I was allowed to eat a chocolate. My daily reward, my discipline.

My friends laughed. Then they asked me why.

"Why don't you dump him? Why do you go on seeing him?"

They added it all up: if that's the way he acts, he doesn't care about you in the least.

"If you love someone, you give yourself completely, without reservations," they kept saying.

It was easy for them, I thought: they gave themselves often, and to many. They needed to love more than they did. They ended up recycling words of love and gift ideas, and weren't even aware of it. If they broke up, they wept, screamed, shouted, then one day . . . they got back on their feet. But if someone like Vittorio came along, who would get back up?

"You forgive him for everything," they added.

They were mistaken: I never forgave Vittorio for anything.

It's just that he protected himself as best he could: from me, from my feelings for him, from the bond that existed between us. Simply put, it was there. Despite the departures, the silences, the cold replies, the walls that went up, the defensive measures, despite the anguish of my expectations that perpetually crumbled. It was there.

And so Vittorio struck back. At times deliberately, at times blindly. But the more we hurt each other, the more evident our miseries, the tighter the knot that bound us.

At that point you either belong to someone or you hold back. I gave myself, he held back. So I lost myself and him in one shot . . .

. . . or are these just lies?

Vittorio left on another trip, but I only learned about it indirectly. After the hospital episode, he simply disappeared.

I tried to look after myself during those days. I couldn't manage it and ultimately, I didn't care.

Then, one morning, I found him down below, leaning against his motorcycle. His face was drawn, there were dark circles under his eyes.

"Haven't you slept?" was the first thing I said to him.

"Am I too complicated?" was his reply.

We're the epitome of eloquence, both of us, I thought. I bit my lip. I shook my head. Don't smile, I ordered myself, don't smile. He breathed out through his nose, his eyes on mine, waiting, and my lips disobeyed.

"What did you do to your finger?" I asked, pointing to the Band-Aid around his fingernail.

"I'm going to pieces," he said, looking at the ground. Then he looked up, and in his eyes there was a sadness that I had never seen.

"Don't worry, I'll put them back together for you."

He hugged me. With my face pressed against his leather jacket, I felt like I couldn't breathe.

THE PERFECT ALMOND TREE
REVELATION

The almond trees were in bloom. Do you know what it's like in the countryside when in February, amid the twisted anguish of the olive trees, the pink-and-white flowers of the almond trees burst forth? They are promises. Acres and acres of promises.

Beneath the dark branches of the almond trees, Antonio saw Silvia dance. She was graceful as she twirled around and laughed, arms outstretched, because the world seemed perfect to her beneath those pink blossoms.

It was already evening. The moon looked down, so yellow. Antonio hadn't known, before then, that an almond grove in bloom, at night, gave off light. Yet there it was, the faint gleam of the white of the buds that smiled in the darkness and with that smile subdued it, conquered it, so that it seemed that even the darkness could not help but make up its mind, finally, to smile. Thus, in that tender light, everything became softer, calmer, more considerate. Gentle, like an old man. How life would be if we could learn how fragile we are. That feelings are fragile. Everything would be bearable, then.

Antonio was enchanted as Silvia danced beneath the flowering almond trees, and so moving was that beauty, the unexpected light, the secret that Silvia was revealing to him, that something inside him shifted. I hadn't understood a thing, Antonio thought; I understand everything now, he said to himself right afterward. But a moment after that, there was no more thinking, just the overwhelming sense of a knot that had been loosened: once he'd stopped tugging at the strings, the knot had come loose with a simple gesture.

26

From: antonia@libero.it
To: vittorioso@gmail.com
Subject: Bougainvilleas on the Lambro

Dear Vittorio,

I had promised myself I would not write to you before you returned. Then I thought that if you don't want to receive any letters during your vacation in India, you simply won't check your e-mail.

Knowing you, you'll open it late in the evening, after coming back from your excursions, when you take off your shoes, toss the socks at the foot of the couch, and light a cigarette. Maybe you even miss having a good cup of coffee. Who knows whether you've been able to find a four o'clock substitute in the meantime.

Knowing you'll find a letter from me, maybe you'll look for my name among the boldface titles of your unread mail, and wonder, Did she resist the temptation? And if I resisted, you'll feel somewhat satisfied, since you are teaching me your way to love, which goes about it by subtraction.

If, on the contrary, I have not resisted, I know you will still be happy to find my name. Because you like to read me. And you like to read me because you love my words more than my left breast, though it is also your favorite. Because you like the image of me writing to you, and the image of you reading me, most of all.

Anyway, listen to what happened to me.

I was with Laura on the banks of the Lambro, early afternoon, as hot as you can imagine. We were watching the river, completely absorbed in its currents that formed swirls and eddies and ripples that ran in opposite directions. At a certain point, a duck. You have to picture this duck just so, which, perched on the water, let itself drift along on the currents. Only the currents were so capricious that the poor creature was driven first right, then left, and when it finally seemed to be able to glide straight ahead, it found itself in a whirlpool and started spinning round and round.

It was so funny! Laura and I laughed harder and harder.

But at some point, as we were laughing at it, the duck made it: it rose up in flight and flew away. Just like that. It looked at us, I'm sure of it, and took off, leaving us there like two assholes, excuse the vulgarity, but it left us there, two human assholes incapable of flying, sitting there gaping, on the bank of the river, in the three o'clock heat.

From: antonia@libero.it
To: vittorioso@gmail.com
Subject: Bougainvilleas and wishes

Vittorio,

Is there something that every night, every blessed night, you dream will happen?

My answer to the question would be yes.

But then I think that time is a funnel and so it doesn't matter, I don't care anymore, even if it doesn't happen. I don't want to spend my life under a funnel, staring up, waiting to see a drop come down. Because staying like that, head back, the blood goes to your head and when you look down, it's all a blank.

I wish my time, now, were a long colorful scarf. I would wind it around my neck and take it for a walk among people, to the hubbub of Piazza Duomo, or the seclusion of the gardens at the Gallery of Modern Art, or to the Ligurian Sea, in the early morning, when a strip of mist is still adrift. And only then would I unwind it and set it down next to me on the bench. To hold your place, in case you want to come when you return.

What a to-do missing you causes.

Antonia

From: antonia@libero.it
To: vittorioso@gmail.com
Subject: Bougainvilleas and reckless actions

He doesn't answer, not him. Did someone write the words "missing you"? Who had the nerve to use the words "missing you"?

But you know what? You can't always be the one to decide everything!

I'm going to have an aperitif at the Navigli. Enough of this.

From: vittorioso@gmail.com
To: antonia@libero.it
Subject: Re: Bougainvilleas and reckless actions

You make me smile. I'm coming back and I have a present for you.

V.

P.S. Beware of Milanese aperitifs: everyone goes to the Navigli pretending it's to have a good time at happy hour. It's really just for the free appetizers.

27

September. I was hoping for the mistral of my region, the crazed sheets twisting round themselves on balcony clotheslines, the sea salt drifting into the houses, white as ever.

Instead, Piacenza's countryside was flat. There was a faint haze on the horizon and a vineyard, where Riccardo was walking with his friends—he was the one who had invited me to his country house that Sunday. We'd known each other since I'd written an article for the magazine he edits. He was forty-five years old and he sent me postcards from around the world. I watched him from the terrace. He picked clusters of grapes, offered a few to his friends.

All you could hear was the braying of donkeys, a tractor in the distance. A barely perceptible wind carried off the colors of summer.

Riccardo looked over at me.

"Come here," he shouted. "We'll take a picture of us!"

We spent the afternoon playing Clue on the porch. I won, unexpectedly; I felt somewhat self-conscious when I announced it and everyone turned to look at me.

Then we strolled through the fields, in small groups, each speaking among themselves. We had put on our fleece jackets. It felt good to be out in the country, in my sneakers, fingernails unpolished. Riccardo gave me a flower.

We came to the oak wood, where the tree trunks had been planted to form a path.

They decided to have a race, whoever arrived at the end first won.

"Anyone who falls starts over again."

The others had already dashed off, one after the other. Only Riccardo and I remained behind; I already had one foot on the mark when he held me back by the arm.

"Are you still seeing Vittorio Solmani?"

I lost my balance and stepped on a dry branch, it snapped.

"I was with him the other night," he continued, "in Milan. There was the presentation of a new imprint, and, anyway, to make a long story short, we had a drink together at the end of the evening."

"Well, he knows that you and I know each other . . ."

"Yes, more or less. He may not know that we're friends, I'm not sure."

"Did something happen?"

Riccardo started to zip up my jacket, I stopped him.

"There's no need, I'm fine."

"I pretended not to know anything about you two, and then, just conversationally, I asked him, 'So, are you seeing anyone?'"

"And?"

Sara slipped when she was almost at the end of the race. "I'm not starting over!" she protested. But she was far away, they were all far away, or so they seemed, covered by the shadows of the woods. Or were we the ones in the dark?

"I bet he said he wasn't seeing anyone!" I said, anticipating the worst and forcing a laugh. It would have been acceptable, it might have been a way to protect me, or maybe . . .

"He said he's seeing two women."

"I don't understand."

"His exact words were, 'Well, right now there are a couple of girls,' and he glossed over it."

"What are you saying, Riccardo?"

The others were calling to us. "You two, talk later!"

"What he told me."

"A couple . . . a couple? Oh my God, it's almost laughable." I turned, my hand over my mouth. "And why would he have told you that? Even if it were true, why? We know each other, he knew you'd tell me."

"I don't think he imagines that we are this close."

The others were laughing. Words such as "moss," "slippery," "penalty" could be heard. Compared to the words "a couple," they were so inoffensive, almost gentle to the ear.

"I don't believe it. He must have had a reason to say that. I know what we are, what he is. Vittorio might be capable of anything, *is* capable of anything, but not such baseness! If he has a virtue, it's sincerity. He's even too sincere. No, if that were the case, he would not have kept it from me."

"Whatever you say."

I hated Riccardo's tone of voice, his flabby belly. What was he thinking, wearing that tight sweater?

"You're a wonderful person, you deserve . . ."

"No, please, don't talk like that."

"Of course."

A magical thought: if one of these tears falls on a red leaf, this entire wood will disappear. I will disappear.

"Did he say anything else?"

"No."

"Dear God."

It was evening when we said good-bye. The cars in the courtyard were ready, we split up, tossed our jackets in the trunk, someone set a tray of leftover focaccias on the backseat.

In the darkness of the countryside, the house, with its glowing skylight, looked like a ship at sea. Someone pointed at the stars. I rubbed my arms, shivering from the cold. Riccardo stood alone, motionless in front of the door, holding the gate's remote control.

When it was my turn to say good-bye, he hugged me tight for a long moment. I clung to that warm, solid body, and for a few seconds I found comfort. But then Riccardo put his mouth to my ear and whispered, "End this relationship. Quickly."

THE PERFECT ALMOND TREE
LIKE A SHIP IN A BOTTLE

De Andrè was singing about the night. Silvia was pinching the dead leaves off the plants in the courtyard and did not know that the song was about a good-bye. So she smiled blissfully at the voice coming from the radio in the living room.

That's how Antonio found her.

"May I?"

"Mama isn't here, but she'll be right back."

"I was looking for you. I brought you a present."

"How nice!" Silvia said excitedly.

"Do you know what it is?"

"No."

"It's a pair of binoculars. They traveled with me for a long time, but now I want you to have them."

He explained that with those she could watch planes in the sky and boats on the sea, that she would be able to see Ruggero coming home before anyone else did, view the roofs of houses or spot birds in the trees. And that they would make distant things seem close.

"I'm leaving, Silvia. I think I can balance on one leg only."

"I won't be able to see you anymore, not even with the binoculars?"
A few days later, Eva packed her bags. She joined Antonio.
"Antonio is gone, Eva is gone."
Ruggero caressed Silvia's hand.
"Do you feel lonely?" he asked.
"I feel like a train station," she replied.
"And what is a train station like?"
"It stands still. It stands still and watches others come and go."

The wind raged along the coast, blowing everything about. The sand whirled up, swept by the mistral, the palm trees were once again bound. And Antonio was no longer there.

"Where's Antonio?" the balconies asked Silvia every morning when they saw her go by. The small loose stones of the streets of San F. crumbled under her heavy but determined footsteps. They no longer dared ask, "Where can we take you, signorina?" The bicycles stood against the walls, the geraniums retreated to their pots.

In the binoculars, life grew large. Silvia was still amazed and covered her father with kisses when he took her with him to discover new scenery to observe. She laughed when she pointed the binoculars at Ruggero from too close up and saw him distorted.

But when the day ended, and she placed the binoculars back in their case, all she wanted to do was close her eyes and sleep. Life went back to being small.

"In my room I fly. I close my eyes and spread my arms. I imagine the sea below me. I do what you used to do, and I seem to feel happy. But you are lost forever. I wish I could close my unfortunate almond eyes and reopen them, knowing that it was all a dream, and that you never flew over our town."

It was a stifling afternoon. The air was heavy with moisture, utterly still. Silvia sought cool relief under the blades of the ceiling fan. The window in her room was open slightly, just enough to see the sun inexorably beat down between the leafy branches of the trees. Another day was ending. Make it stop, Silvia wanted to say, and maybe, barely whispering it, she did. What would she remember before falling asleep? Days shouldn't be able to end if they haven't had some meaning. Give them another chance. Give me another chance, Silvia thought, maybe I will have the strength to get up from this bed and go looking for him, just like that, I'll step out of the house, and when my mother sees me at the door and asks me where I'm going, I'll tell her, "I'm going to look for Antonio." Like that, simply. Because the biggest things are perhaps also the simplest. And going to look for him would be a big thing. But Silvia did not move from her bed, she knew that she was the station, the cradle, the bay. She was as still as that oppressive August air. Where could a girl with almond-shaped eyes go?

Breakfast at eight. Snack at ten. Lunch at one. Another snack at five. Supper at eight. How are you? Fine, thanks. What did you see today? The walls of my house, the square of sky from the window, the bit of sea that flows in front of the beach. The usual horizons. They say that each day we can change our lives. And maybe it's true, but not for everyone. Because if life were made to be changed each day, why then did God make some of us capable of grasping the moment, of turning the world on its head, of dropping everything and running off, whereas others he bound to a piece of land, to a wheelchair, to a man? They say that life is ours. What a gross lie.

"So, Silvia, the world has begun to turn the way we didn't want it to," old Amilcare whispered, sitting down beside her on the last bench along the promenade.

Silvia's feet did not reach the ground, and she swung her red ballerina shoes.

"Don't look for the exact moment when it happened, there's no such thing, it just happens. And don't believe it when they tell you that you must be getting big, because getting big has nothing to do with it. Rather it's becoming little, very little, invisible even to ourselves."

"But does it end? This sadness, I mean, does it end?"

28

Vittorio would keep his hands in his pockets, and meanwhile he seemed to be tossing words up in the air, letting them circle round, then catching them, like a juggler handling three balls. His words had no need of gestures to push them, they were swings, always high up, and if you sat on them, with the tip of your shoe you could touch the sky . . .

Today too I cried over him. His blue eyes. That brief movement as he raised his head slightly, his gaze resting on me, then there they were, under the long lashes, those blue eyes.

I was on the bus, and sitting in front of me was an elderly gentleman with a cap on his head, a shopping bag, and a beatific, vacant smile.

I would have liked to be his age as well: quench the fires, surrender to losses with a shrug, make peace with life. Know that the battle is over and the result doesn't matter, it's over. Now you can buy a yellow canary and feed it at six in the morning, you can put on a cap and go to the fruit market, buy a couple of peaches, caress their fuzzy skin, get on a bus and observe the city from the window, feeling only the gentleness of life as it flows. Not be bothered by a girl who's crying.

But when I got off the bus, I was still young and I still loved Vittorio. With Vittorio it will never end. It's like a city you always end up going back to.

Day Seven: Let the mixture rest without stirring.

"How the hell dare they talk about me?"

Bar della Rinascente. We were on the terrace, and the spires of the Duomo were so close that it was impossible to keep my eyes on Vittorio without continuously shifting my gaze.

And meanwhile there was Silvia, you can believe me, Silvia was there leaping from one spire to another and waving in my direction.

"Look, I'm not a silly little fool who questions every single thing the first time she hears a bit of gossip. I'm here, and I trust you. That's why I'm telling you about this story of Riccardo."

Vittorio brooded nervously, retracing his confidential exchanges with Riccardo, the pats on the back. He shook his head no. But as to whether the statement was true or not, not a word.

Silvia, on the spire, watched me. "What are you doing there?" she said. "There's nothing for you there."

"Well, I mean, what am I supposed to think?" I burst out, then.

Vittorio raised his eyes to me. Two small furrows formed on his forehead. There, that was his expression when striking: Vittorio looked at you sadly, as if it weren't up to him, as if, deep down, he had no other choice. He had such a way of wounding you . . . You fell apart in front of him, and Vittorio looked at you with an all-consuming sorrow.

"Yes, I told him that," he said clearly. "I told him that I have a couple of women."

Silvia was staring at me, balancing on the spire on one foot only.

"But it's not true," he added.

"I'd better go."

"It's not true."

"Then why, can you explain it to me? Why say such a thing?"

"To mislead him."

"Now you're going to tell me that you did it to protect me?"

"I just don't go around talking about my affairs. I didn't want to talk about us."

"But why can't you talk about us? Why? And how can I believe you?"

"You're free to believe the first one who comes along, in that case."

I closed my eyes, breathed deeply. Walk away from here, Antonia, walk away.

Vittorio leaned toward me.

"Make me a promise."

"A promise? Me?"

I knew he would never take my hands, but instinctively I withdrew them. There was still time to get away.

"You know who I am perhaps better than I myself know," he began, and everything in the background seemed to disappear: the red of the sunset, the waiters coming and going, the laughter of friends, those who maybe, one day, away from him, I too might find.

"Promise me that if today, or tomorrow, you see enemies around me, you'll tell me. Promise me that you won't believe what others say, promise me that you'll always be on my side."

"I don't understand what you're saying, Vittorio."

"Defend me."

He said, "Defend me." Vittorio Solmani, the brilliant, well-to-do, esteemed publisher, said this to me, huddled there in my chair, in my cheap little dress, my badly drawn eyebrows, with a book of "women's" poetry, as he'd called it, in my handbag. With my desire to run off, to forget, with the atrocious doubt—the certainty, all in all—of not being loved.

"Defend me."

At one time I believed that love was a gift. Instead, you pay for everything, piece by piece.

I promised. I would always, no matter what, be on Vittorio Solmani's side.

That day on the terrace of Bar della Rinascente, I promised, and Silvia went away. When I turned to look for her on the spires, she was gone.

29

Pussyfoot around his feelings. Don't try to break his silences. Don't expect to overcome his fears. Don't force him to confront them. Don't ask anything of him, love makes no demands. Don't let him feel the weight of your expectations. Don't disturb him, but remind him that you are there. Remind him that you're there, but without disturbing him. Be frivolous and be substantial. Act like a guest in his life, one should enter the lives of others on tiptoe. Knock at his heart, but do it lightly and only once in a blue moon. Slip a note under the door, ask permission. Have your coat and umbrella ready, wait. Your love is great, but make sure it is not intrusive. Love can be terribly intrusive, it's a tyrannical, overbearing feeling. Let him feel free, pretend you feel just as free.

If he doesn't see the problem, if he tells you, "This is who I am, take it or leave it," if he tramples your feelings like an elephant, if you feel your heart fall to pieces a thousand times, pick up the pieces a thousand times and hide them from his eyes. He'll believe that you are still whole, that you don't feel the pain he's caused you. Pick up the pieces, repair them, start again.

If you memorized a love poem that begins with "Yesterday I kissed you on the lips" and you learned it just to be able to murmur it to him after lovemaking, breathing the words on his flushed face, pressed to his skin that still tastes of your skin, if all you want is to whisper it to him in the dark and in return have him kiss your ear with his hot breath and his laugh and his teeth gleaming in the night, don't do it: go on lying there on him, and as you trace a finger over his face, his nose, his cheekbones and lips, especially the lips, recite it in your mind. Yesterday I kissed you on the lips . . .

If you can't get to sleep when he's sleeping beside you, because you think that you've never had anything so beautiful and that you would change all your plans for this thing and that it would not be the reckless sacrifice that he fears, but the luckiest trade that fate can offer you, don't wake him up to tell him that, don't hug him tight, don't rest your forehead on the back of his neck as your body is crying out to do, losing yourself in the scent of his hair, don't so much as touch him. Trace his profile, finger hovering, and in the air sketch the caress you don't dare make. Hold in the feeling that spills over, that robs you of breath and sleep and the contours of the night. Count the moles on his back. Thirty-nine, the number of Vittorio's moles. Thirty-nine, the number of stifled "I love yous."

30

A pool. Night. Liguria. A beach chair with its white-and-green-striped cushions, the yellow glow of a garden light in the shrubbery. At the edge of the pool, a dark patch. The motionless profile of pines. Then a moth brushed the water. Something stirred: the leaves, an animal, or the night itself. A tolling of bells in the distance, once, twice. Two o'clock.

I dipped my foot in, just a little; I drew it back. My white nightgown, the silk gleaming in the dark.

The villa where we were staying as guests was on a terraced cliff overlooking the sea. Above me now were bedrooms with flower-filled balconies, their lights turned off; and below, beyond the rose gardens, a rock-filled sea. A calm, silent sea. Sure it was still there?

I looked up at our balcony, the curtains of the room wide open—Vittorio too loved waking up to the light of day—and I felt afraid that it might all end, the scent of his skin, the insane traveling, my sheer joy.

A few nights earlier, the landlady had come by to pick up the final rent and asked me whether I intended to stay on in Milan. My work was nearly finished, I could repack my bags and go home. But I had bought some time: "I'd like one more month, for the time being."

Now I was in that villa in Liguria, so beautiful as to think my presence there was a mistake, and there were the stars, which did not seem distant to me. Besides, distance seemed like a nice place to be. Even those meters between me and Vittorio that night, between my legs, puckered by goose bumps, at the edge of a pool and the window beyond which his warm body lay between the sheets; even those few meters seemed full of nocturnal fragrances, of thoughts, of possibilities. My heart was brimming with possibilities.

Yet that same day, while we were looking for the way to Ivonne's house, we'd stopped to wash the motorcycle, and I, trying to hold the hose, had ended up giving Vittorio and me a shower. I giggled like a child, and he too had laughed, I'm not saying he didn't, but he'd immediately grabbed the pump out of my hand and continued by himself: "Put more coins in, please."

He doesn't love me, I thought. The cry of an owl hoo-hooed in the darkness. It's just that on nights like those, I felt that my love would be enough for both of us. I knew it wasn't true, but I wanted to be stronger than the truth.

A train passed, the tracks ran along the sea, very close. It made quite a racket. I glanced toward Vittorio's room: would he have been awakened?

Now I wanted to go back up, slip into bed beside him, press myself against his body, say, "Vittorio, I'm cold," see if, befuddled by sleep, he would hug me.

Even though I knew that if I returned to that bedroom, I'd lose all my dreams, all my thoughts, my way of looking at things, of listening, of speaking my mind, my favorite position to sleep in, the amount of salt I put in the pasta; everything would be decided by him. Love fills and drains you with the same brutality.

I rested my forehead on my knees. The truth was that I had no idea what to do.

We stayed a few days at Ivonne's house on the coast. When I came upon her in the kitchen, amid the linguine with shellfish and fried calamari, I placed a hand lightly on her arm.

"I wanted to thank you for your hospitality, I haven't had a chance to till now. It's lovely being here."

"My pleasure, there's always been room for Vittorio's girlfriends."

Ivonne had big green eyes, properly accented with liberal strokes of black pencil, sharp facial features, a hooked nose, thin lips, but the broad smile of a frog. She had a pageboy cut, with short bangs, and a skinny body. She wore several rings on her fingers. She hugged everyone, often, going from room to room with nervous gestures. She was the daughter of a building contractor.

"But my mother paints, her one-man exhibitions have had great success in New York, and she writes poetry."

She had a passion for kimonos and spritzers. She must have been just a few years older than I was, but it was she who had chosen the *tansu* pieces so prominent in the rooms, and arranged for them to be shipped from the island of Hokkaido; that was enough to create distance between me and her.

Above all, she "knew people." She opened the doors of her house, planned lunches and dinners, was constantly preparing beds, or sofa beds when all the beds were taken. Every day was a flurry of friends of all nationalities.

The eccentricity of the people coming and going from that house amused me: I laughed at Damiano who knocked at our rooms at night, wearing one of Ivonne's kimonos, his eyes made up à la japonaise. I laughed when Vittorio, before falling asleep, counted how many bones there were in the house that night.

"Two hundred and six multiplied by five people equals what, Antonia?"

At the table there was a volley of reciprocal questions: what do you do, what's your view of that issue in your country, but what do you think of . . . I listened, at first, with the same fervor to know, understand, inquire. I strained to translate when they spoke English, nodding my head enthusiastically. I thought about Sunday dinners at my house:

"Do you like this sauce? Did you have some? Want seconds?" I thought, I never want to go back.

But then I quickly got distracted—how beautiful everyone's hair was when the sunlight shone on it. And our shadows on the white wall, look, there's one of my curls—I drifted on the surface of their international discussions.

I should interject, I should say something too (who was that silent girl trailing along behind Vittorio Solmani?). Instead, I kept quiet. With some embarrassment, I realized that I had almost emptied my plate while the others, engrossed in the discussion, still had full plates in front of them. I slowed down the act of bringing the fork to my mouth, I concentrated on that, on adjusting my pace. Everyone forgot my presence.

Ivonne, on the other hand, spoke constantly about the short film she was working on. From her smartphone, she read several lines that she had already drafted.

"I can't conceive of TV's turning literature into a show, I can't accept such a thing." She leaned over the table, wineglass gripped like a weapon. "Writing is such an intimate act!"

Later on she planned an outing for an aperitif.

After supper each evening, as he was slipping off his shoes, Vittorio would talk about how interesting he had found P's theory and how he fully supported V's project. Certainly, if he needed someone in that field, he would turn to N. Then too, had I heard what an incredible life T had lived?

Vittorio had something to say about everyone: that one was brilliant, another was a person of infinite culture, another so funny, she brought you to tears.

About Dorotea, who occupied the room next to ours, he remarked, "She's an extraordinary woman, an intense woman." I don't know what I would have given to hear him describe me that way. An intense woman. But I had no name, there was no way I could have any adjectives.

From their hands projects flourished.

From an hour's conversation, during afternoons on the beach, sitting cross-legged on black rocks, festivals took shape, along with sponsors, contacts, publicity slogans. And while Damiano went crabbing and proudly displayed his haul to us, holding them by the shell, their ideas, like waves, followed in rapid succession, tumbling out, surging ever forward.

Occasionally Vittorio alluded to my writing, but I, doubting that he wanted to show that there was something interesting about me as well, immediately retreated from the conversation. I plunged back into silence, catching the questioning looks of the others, and sensed a dark shadow all around me.

Then they dove from the highest cliff and took long swims. Vittorio shouted to me, "Coming?" And I, paralyzed on my ridiculous pink towel, called back, "I'll join you later." He turned his back to the shore and swam toward the others. I stayed behind, watching the cruel spectacle of the crabs fighting among themselves in the bucket.

The fact is that I thought they all swam better than me. That they all spoke better than me. That what filled my hours was merely a marginal aspect of existence. The important thing was reading the right magazines, proving you were curious. Dressing casually but with unique accessories. Laughing and drinking a lot, even when you didn't feel like it. Asking, "Have you read the latest . . . ?" Or prefacing a remark with "I met . . . ," at times exploring the financial circumstances of the others' activities with ill-concealed spite: "What is your reaction to . . . ?" and replying with lies or a witty remark accompanied by another sip of wine. Appearing bizarre enough to be considered interesting. Offering a cigarette. "Antonia?" "I don't smoke, thank you." And always seeming very sure of what you say.

I felt small, insignificant, plodding. In a word, an outsider.

While the others worked on plans for a festival, all I did was study and read newspapers. I took the bike that Ivonne had lent me and rode to the newsstand in town, I would buy magazines in Italian, French,

English, and walk along, holding them under my arm, glancing at the covers, anticipating the pleasure of releasing them from the cellophane and leafing through them—before abandoning them in the magazine rack, drawn back by a book of poetry. Still, with those magazines under my arm, I liked myself, I felt like I was walking on air. I acquired an identity.

Instead, I was appropriating one. But I wanted to be able to take part in the conversations.

They raised issues I'd been unaware of until then: political, social, economic. I began to understand what the newspapers were writing about, what the politicians on talk shows were arguing about, drowning one another out with such fury.

"There's Antonia, she's finally opening up," Vittorio exclaimed.

But where was I? Where was I really?

I was in libraries where I shut myself up for days, reading about the life of a writer. I was in the hours I spent writing. I was in the lure of a book of poetry while the news aired on TV, in the emotion that a line of verse left me when I read it for the first time, and for a moment the heart found itself caught and remained so, as if snared by an invisible hook. I was in an imaginary place called San F., with a girl with Down syndrome who never existed but to whom I felt close. I was that girl.

I would have to stop being one of those women for whom life is tolerable only with the delusion of imagination, I would have to "transform my anxiety from emotional to intellectual," as Vittorio put it, and "make way for new life experiences."

But what was I without my fabrications? The essential, evident truths that Vittorio held out to me would never be enough for me.

"One should always be wary of people who presume to know how to love."

So Vittorio declared.

We were in the living room with Dorotea, the intense young Slavic woman. She had a mole on her wrist, a detail that constantly distracted me from her words. She gesticulated, and that little spot moved with her, dark against her alabaster skin; it turned up on the blue sofa, grazed the white walls, seemed to want to make a leap and free itself from that wrist.

From the large window overlooking the pool, we watched autumn remind us of its existence, after days of heat and sun exceptional for early October. Fat drops of rain plopped against the windows, the tops of the pines tried to huddle close, the branches holding one another tight, yet they frayed and their needles scattered over the pool.

Dorotea had spoken to me and Vittorio about her companion, shut up in his office all day, who was grudging with time and tenderness.

"I don't think he loves me as much as I love him."

I held my breath, dreading Vittorio's reply.

"One should always be wary of people who presume to know how to love."

Dorotea took off her glasses.

"Why?" she asked.

"Because, and you're a demonstration of it, they are the ones ready to point a finger at you, to issue judgments. They accuse you of everything you should do for them and don't do—they have preprinted lists, always right at hand—whereas they would do anything for you."

"Sometimes, though, it's true," I managed to argue in a faint voice.

"You can't be so ingenuous!" Vittorio exploded. "Tell me you don't really believe that!"

He laughed and raised his eyes toward heaven, sitting there in front of me and Dorotea, who had shrunk back into the sofa, as far away as possible from his words. From the armchair, his legs spread, Vittorio leaned toward us: take and drink from it, this is the cup of bitterness.

"That's not love, Antonia, it's a constant expectation on the shoulders of the one who is the object of that feeling. Giving oneself totally can be romantic, moving, undoubtedly. But it depletes both the one who experiences that feeling and the one who is its object."

"Do you think he shares your opinion?" Dorotea asked. "Be honest, Vittorio."

I turned to the young woman. Surely you don't believe him! Don't agree with him, answer back, say something, you smile every time you get a message from the man you love, you put on your best dress on the day of his birthday, you know it isn't so.

"I don't know. Some people are made for living, and others are made for loving. I know what I think: for me being loved like that is not desirable. And it's dishonest to love like that."

"Dishon . . . ?"

My legs were trembling. Dorotea instinctively glanced over at me. And you—her eyes were telling me—don't you have anything to say?

I got on the bicycle, it was still raining. I pedaled absurdly. The state road, the curves along sheer cliffs dropping to the sea, the slippery asphalt. Then the steep descent toward town, bell towers soaring against the gray, the sound of the wheels on the pavement, the faulty brakes, unexpected crossroads. Run, run toward the sea, that leaden expanse. Close your eyes, smell the fragrances, the rain, the looming forest, the falling leaves—I too want to fall.

Face it, this is what it is, this is the love I feel for him. This thing that in my eyes is precious and clean and beautiful, for him is a monster that suffocates him, a constant demand that I, albeit not explicitly, make of him. Something dishonest.

A bus, ominously, blares its horn—you have a stop sign!—the sound of leaves crushed under the wheels. Finally this summer is over, this charade of trips to the beach and ice cream cones on the way home.

So is there a different way, is there a "generous" way to love? Can I go on loving him without asking for anything in return? I can. Of course I can. Hide my feelings, swallow my words, stifle my expectations, rule out demands, ignore disappointments—I've been doing that for months. But for what? The truth is that I was simply waiting, just waiting all this time for something to change, for him to wake up next to me one morning and realize that it was me, it was me who'd made his life better, and then something would thaw.

You can't be so ingenuous, I thought. Tell me you don't really believe that!

The sign marking the entrance to town reads:

BENVENUTI, WILLKOMMEN, BIENVENUE

THIS MUNICIPALITY HAS TEN BELL TOWERS

But how many crossroads are there, why don't you write that?

I, at each one of them that day, prayed that a car might speed past and take me with it, one instant and that would be it. Maybe then Vittorio would notice that I too existed in that relationship.

But look here, Antonia—as you fail to brake, picturing the pathetic, shameful image of a hospital bed with Vittorio at your bedside—listen up: Vittorio was right. Wouldn't throwing yourself under a car be a terrible act against him, an atrocious form of blackmail, something light-years away from love? So it's true, even your love is a monster.

31

I watched couples dancing a waltz under the arcades. It was a night in Genoa. A short walk from the boisterous, trendy pubs where small groups of young people stood on the sidewalk with beers in their hands, a small band was playing a waltz, and men and women in evening clothes whirled around. They were so lovely. In a timeless dimension.

If I were asked what might be hiding around the corner, I would say that one day I found a band playing a waltz there, where I would never have imagined it.

"Vittorio, I drew a picture of you." I handed him the sheet of paper.

"But I'm hanging from a moving train!"

"Is it enough like Indiana Jones?"

"More than enough. It's fantastic. You're my Aladdin's lamp."

But does the genie in Aladdin's lamp have wishes? And if she did, what would they be?

Maybe that someone would stop always expecting something from her. That they would stop rubbing her and try caressing her sometimes. That before telling her their wishes, they would ask, "What are yours?" That those wishes might be forever, and not just for a moment. That someone would leave her in peace, at least occasionally, and let her dream about wishes that would not for once need lamps to grant them, and would be no less real as a result. Because those wishes too are real, the ones that are impossible.

He withdrew in silence, in Genoa. Piazza delle Erbe was swarming with people, Vittorio and I were having an aperitif outdoors. I sipped mine often; putting my face in the glass gave me comfort. I had tried to joke: Vittorio had managed a strained smile. I kept quiet, waiting for him to regain his space: he'd buried his head in the newspapers. I fluffed up my freshly cut hair, unrolled the scarf I wore around my neck, leaving my cleavage visible. He hadn't deigned to look at me. I reached my hand out on the table, casually—it would have taken so little—it stayed there. Then I asked him if everything was all right.

"Why shouldn't it be?"

He told me about all the times he had dined at the restaurant overlooking the piazza with those people I knew and how wonderful those evenings were, endlessly arguing until dawn. He yawned loudly. He finished the pretzels in the bowl before I could taste one, answered his phone. Crushed, all I could do was stare at the red of the aperitif, ignoring the friendly tone his voice immediately assumed on the phone, the note of contentment he reserved for the caller who had interrupted us. Was it perhaps relief?

"Are you sure there's nothing wrong?"

"What do you want from me?" he replied sharply.

"I want you not to answer me that way, to begin with."

"You've been hassling me with these questions all evening."

"You've been impossible all day. Why are you irritable?"

"Now I am. Before I was just fine."

He threw the money to cover the bill on the table and stood up. I hadn't yet finished my drink. That's how he was, Vittorio: he thought he could decide everything, when to sit, when to get up, when you could be happy, and when it was time for you to swallow all the poison he dished out to you.

We headed toward a bar where his friends were waiting for us. We walked along, each of us distant. The *carruggi* seemed steep and dark.

"So, tell me, why so unhappy?" he asked.

"Oh, I'm the one who's unhappy? Vittorio, we've been going around for hours, and you've done nothing but keep to yourself. If I weren't there, it would have been all the same to you."

"What do you want from me? You want me to kiss you on the neck every five minutes?"

I froze. After a few seconds, realizing that I wasn't following him, he turned around. He looked at me, waiting for me to budge or say something.

"Fuck you," I said.

"What?"

"Fuck you."

I turned on my heel and walked away.

"You're really a shit," I muttered under my breath.

"Very mature of you, congratulations. A couple of remarks and you walk off. Come back here, if you have something you want to settle."

"And what do you expect me to settle with someone like you? A man who hasn't understood a thing about me. Who tells me, 'You want me to kiss you every five minutes?' Go ahead, go to your friends, I don't feel like it."

"You're acting like a little child."

"So what, that's what you think of me. And if you don't like my company, don't invite me out anymore."

"Why do you always act like the offended one? For Christ's sake, there's nothing more unbearable than people who constantly feel offended, by life, by others, it's insufferable."

A punch in the gut. Was it true?

"There you are!" Damiano appeared. "The others are already at the bar, shall we go together?"

"Right, we were just headed there," Vittorio replied, peremptorily motioning me to follow them.

"So then, do we want to make peace?" he asked some hours later, as soon as the bedroom door closed behind us. "Come on, come here and give me a kiss to make up."

I went, he hugged me.

"Why the hell must you always think I have a low opinion of you?" he asked.

We made love, I felt his wine breath on my face the whole time. He turned off the light and dropped off.

At dawn, I slipped out of bed, crept into the shower, and cried, my arms braced against the blue tiles. When I went back to the bedroom, his naked body lay at an angle, taking up all the space in the bed. Legs spread-eagle, arms outstretched, he left not so much as an inch for me. I hated him.

32

He kissed me, but he never held my hand. He made love, but then he closed his eyes, and it was as if I were already gone.

Nevertheless, I chose to change my plans for Vittorio, to rearrange my life so I could remain in Milan. Without ever telling him that it was for him.

"What about your projects?" Gioia asked me.

"I'll move them to another city."

"It's not the same thing, you know. And your family?"

"They'll always be there."

"And your town? You love your town."

"I'll have a place to come back to."

"But . . ."

"But nothing. People move."

"Shouldn't you ask him if he wants you to turn your life upside down for him, beforehand?"

"He would say no, even if he wanted me to—he would never accept that responsibility."

"But he should. You should accept that responsibility together. You have to tell him. He has to know that you're changing your life for him."

"Absolutely not!"

"You're only doing this because you're afraid he'll tell you not to."

"I'm doing it because I love him, and I know he's incapable of assuming responsibility for a person's happiness or unhappiness."

"It's unfair to him."

"On the contrary, I'm doing it out of love, so he won't feel coerced, so he won't have to bear the burden of my expectations and my decisions."

"No, you're doing it because you're afraid he doesn't love you enough to want you to stay."

"If he didn't want me with him, he'd leave me."

"In fact you're not a couple. For Christ's sake, Antonia, think, use your head! You're giving up everything for a man who can't even say that you're a couple!"

"I've already made up my mind. Now, please, let's not talk about it anymore."

But one night, while we were having dinner, Vittorio asked me, "Why not try to look for work in other cities?"

I remember the indifference in his eyes. The cool imperturbability as he poured himself more wine and brought the napkin to his mouth, awaiting my reply. The height from which I plummeted.

"Where?"

I listened to a list of cities pour from his lips: far away, all far from Milan.

"At this point I'm going back home," I said in one breath, without looking at him.

"But in fact you never told me why you don't want to go back anymore."

The conversation didn't seem real. Suddenly everything was absurd. A joke in bad taste.

"Do you want to have some new experiences?" he suggested.

"That's right, I want to have some new experiences," I agreed, then I left my fork on my plate and didn't touch another mouthful.

33

"Go home, Antonia."

Vittorio chose the telephone to tell me. It was evening, it was late. We had argued over something silly. I had asked him to join me at Gioia's the next day, I wanted to introduce her to him, and he, once again, had refused. I'd raised my voice a little, he had maintained his cogent, dismissive tone to tell me that he was still free to choose whom he felt like meeting.

"Vittorio, it was nothing. Why such a reaction?"

That's when he issued his sentence.

"Go home, Antonia. Go back to your city."

"I . . . I don't want to go home."

The phone's battery was low, so I was crouched on the floor, in the living room, with the phone plugged into the outlet. The only light on was the one in the bedroom, a faint glow spilled into the hallway and stopped there.

"You want to send me away?"

A long silence.

"I don't want to send you away, but you need to make a life for yourself. It's not fair otherwise."

"I *am* making a life!"

"That's not true. You had other plans when I met you, other aspirations."

"I'm doing what I want for myself now. Why do you want me to leave?"

"I can't do this, Antonia, I'm sorry. I can't do it."

"You can't do what?"

"I'm not someone whose feelings run away with him. You . . ."

"Me? I haven't asked you for anything, Vittorio. I haven't asked you for a thing!"

More silence. The room in darkness. I stared, but all I saw were shadows. The room where we had danced together.

"You would always be disappointed by me."

"I don't understand what you're saying, Vittorio. I'm trying, I swear, but I don't understand."

"As long as you expect something from me, you'll be disappointed. You should be happy. Listen to me, listen carefully: staying with me won't make you happy. I want you to be happy, truly."

"But I'm happy here, there's nowhere else, there's no other way!"

"Why are you doing this, Antonia?"

"Doing what? Vittorio, I . . . You're the most . . . unexpected and beautiful thing that has ever happened to me. I didn't choose you; if I'd had a choice, I would probably not have chosen you. But this is a greater force, incomprehensible and yet . . . beautiful. So beautiful. And I don't care if I have to upset my plans, toss them out the window, change everything. I made up my mind to bow to this feeling, I . . . I'd be crazy not to do it."

I felt him smile at the phone.

"Are you laughing?"

"No, I'm not laughing."

"Did you smile?"

"Yep."

"You smiled because what I said was a beautiful thing."

"Yeah."

The arm of the sofa was in front of me, with its flowered upholstery. What I wanted to do now was end the call and lie down on those lilac-colored lilies, nurse the sense of emptiness. But my ear was attached to the phone, hanging on every sound: now every breath would be a reply.

Abruptly, Vittorio became aggressive.

"No, Antonia. I mean it, no. I don't want anyone to change her life for me. Anyone's mood to depend on mine. I don't want that."

"But how is that a problem? Can you tell me what's really the problem? Are you in love with someone else?"

"No."

"An old flame from the past?"

"What? No, no."

"So all you wanted to do was take me to bed?"

"Don't talk bullshit. You're offensive when you say such shitty things."

"Then what is it? You tell me, what is it?"

I felt a desperate fury, for me, for him, for that last match we were playing and losing, for everything that was slipping away, that I had nurtured, cared for, tried to hold on to with every resource I had.

"This is not a game, Vittorio, this is my life, our life. It's not a game."

"Exactly, if you want to disrupt your life for me, don't do it."

In the silence of the room, only the ticking of the clock on the wall; it was by that ticking, during all those months, that I had measured the minutes of loneliness, of Vittorio's absences, of waiting for him to return.

"I would have done it. I would have done anything to stay with you. But I can't force you."

"No," he said. "It's I who can't force you."

"So all you wanted to do was take me to bed," I whispered, drained.

"Is that what you want me to say? Is that it? Is it? Then I'll say it. I don't love you, Antonia."

As my back slid along the wall and my body sank to the ground, all I could think of was how beautiful the words "I love you" sounded on his lips, how wonderful it would have been to hear them without that negative in between.

In that moment that had lost the contours of time, in the dark room where I would cry until the first morning light, my ridiculous heart had only that one thought: how beautiful "I love you" spoken by Vittorio sounded.

THE PERFECT ALMOND TREE
NEVER AGAIN

"Ease this knot, Lord. I beg You, make it all stop. Songs, stop playing. Poetry, stop reciting. Planes, stop flying. I implore You, put out this fire, snuff it out, before I lose my mind. It will never end. Never."

"May the grace of the Lord be with you always."

"And with thy spirit."

The last light of day came faintly through the stained-glass windows of the little church of Sant'Oronzo. It had been a muggy day, and the chapel still held its heat. The few faithful were scattered among the pews, fanning themselves with the leaflets for the liturgy.

"I ask only one thing, Lord. Only one thing, and then I won't ask for anything more in my whole life. Now I know what I want, and I won't ask for anything else. Even when I'm old and alone, Lord, I won't ask You for anything. But hear me now."

The prie-dieu was hard, but that slight pressure on the kneecaps seemed necessary to Silvia, like a price to pay to see her prayer answered.

The organist played the final hymn, and an elderly woman accompanied him with a well-known song that filled the church. Silvia's eyes were closed, squeezed tight.

"Make them all disappear, Lord. I'm begging You, I implore You. Make it so not a single one remains on Earth."

The choir stopped.

"The Mass is ended. Go in peace."

"Thanks be to God."

The faithful welcomed Don Felice's blessing with relief, since it allowed them to go back to the fans in their homes, and as if suddenly awakened from a stupor, they left the pews and headed toward the door, now almost in a hurry.

Not so Silvia, who remained kneeling.

"Now I'm opening my eyes, Lord. I'm getting up, I'm going to leave this church, and when I'm outside, they won't be there anymore. That's right, isn't it, Lord? Yes, now I'll go outside, and there will be no more almond trees. Never again."

"Silvia, shall we go?"

Slowly she opened her eyes, stood up, leaning on her mother, and walked down the narrow aisle of the church. And with every step, she felt lighter and lighter, because her prayer would be answered, she felt it. God would not disappoint her and, beyond the church door, there would be a new world, with no more almond trees, and no other Silvias: a happy world. She would be the last girl with almond-shaped eyes, the last not to be loved by a man like Antonio.

She made the sign of the cross, winking at Jesus on the cross. Her heart was pounding as she went down the steps to the churchyard and looked up at the surrounding countryside. She was already smiling, because, she was sure of it now, God would not let her down.

A gust of cool wind blew through the town.

"The mistral, Signora Maria, tomorrow we'll breathe!"

"Let's hope so, Signor Franco. Good night."

"Good night to you too! *Ciao*, Silvia!"

Silvia remained silent.

"Silvia, don't you answer?"

More silence.

"Silvia, what's wrong? Why are you crying? Silvia, sweetheart, what are you looking at?"

"The almond trees."

34

A steep slope, these blank pages.

At every step, you lose your footing. Don't fall, I tell myself.

The words appear, hide, reveal themselves. They are never the right ones.

Don't fall, I tell myself again. Instead, I plunge into things. Into the depths of feelings. Where it is so dark and so bottomless that words won't come.

I cannot. I retreat. I want to write for Silvia, silently waiting for someone to shape her steps, relay her dreams, give her a before and an after, a conclusion.

But the blank pages are steep, like these streets I walk along, like Vittorio's rejection, which has become rejection by the world, like the silence that has formed around me since the day I left. Like the certainties I saw dissolve, the ideas I heard knock that I never thought I would accept, like my yes to change, said too soon and too loudly.

I don't know anymore. What the visceral love for life is, which I am nevertheless unable to live. Whether it's true that Antonio can return to Silvia and find the meaning of it all in her almond eyes and those of individuals like her. Whether Eva will really be able to travel the world and be happy. I don't know anymore.

And so the pen marks only a dot on the sheet before being raised; undecided, it remains suspended. So, is the time for the written word over?

From: vittorioso@gmail.com
To: antonia@libero.it
Subject:

Antonia, I miss you. And I know I'll go on missing you. But I have no choice. After all, it wasn't my decision.

V.

After reading this message, I called Vittorio. He didn't answer. I wrote to him. I wrote again. I tried to reach him, desperately, stubbornly. Nothing rushes to meet its ruin more quickly than a feeling that is mortified yet ready to leap at any sign of hope.

"When I met you," Vittorio said, "when we started seeing each other, I didn't think that this thing between us would become what it is. I didn't expect it to become important, and now . . ."
"Now?"
"Now I'm in a panic."
"Why?"
"I like my life the way it is. I don't want it to change."
"But everything can't be like your four o'clock coffee or the Sunday morning fruit shake, you realize that, don't you?"
"I don't want to lose my freedom, nothing is more important to me."
"But don't you see that there's another kind of freedom, which you are giving up? The freedom to embrace a feeling. To allow your plans to be upset. To let your guard down, for once. That too is freedom,

and what do you do instead? You shut yourself up in a cage of habits and certainties, you hide behind your image as a 'free spirit.' But what is a free man, Vittorio? Someone who says, 'I miss you, but I have no choice'? Is that a free man?"

"I really need to think about it."

"Think about it, then. Because the way it is, I can't take it anymore."

"It's all or nothing?"

"No, it's a request to acknowledge a feeling."

We parted.

God, I beg You, enlighten his heart. Let him understand what he feels for me, whatever it may be, because I can't hold up any longer.

Silvia? Silvia? Take me to the sea. Bring me your open laughter, the new name of a flower, your solid roots, the beauty of how unguarded you are, with no need to erect defenses.

35

Now, now I just want to finish telling this story. Rush to the conclusion, strip off all the tattered shreds of life. No longer have to sift through the past, relive the colors of those days, experience everything all over again: the delusions, transports, loneliness, anguish. Enough.

And when I think of all the times, walking by myself through this city, I imagined seeing him coming toward me, a shopping bag in hand, a distracted look . . . I think it's time to put an end to something so overwhelming. And hope to never experience it again.

Day Eight: Let the mixture continue to rest without stirring.

This inert batter, sealed in a bowl for days, looking at me.

And me, looking at myself in the mirror. Every night.

There is a woman in the world who every night watches her body fade; who, in front of the mirror, observes the sagging flesh, the lusterless skin, the advancing wrinkles. And it wouldn't be so bad if that person weren't thinking, There, if he had accepted my offer, earlier on

I could have given him my youthful breasts, my firm arms, my curvaceous hips. Instead, the rejected gift slowly perishes, and what remains of the splendor of a day—the golden color of the skin, the sinuous forms—is merely sorrow clinging to bones.

That woman, Vittorio, wonders whether it isn't a sin to love and not be loved, to be loved and not love. To let the days of our lives go by without caressing a taut belly, a soft neck, nights without a body to cuddle up to in the cold. And tell oneself, "Life goes on"—sure, it goes on, albeit briefly—and sure, "Life is more than that," life contains so many things that if we could experience them all, we'd go mad—and forget. How can we forget?

He came back to me. Vittorio knocked at my door. Standing in the doorway, his eyes smiling, all he said was, "This time I'm not late."

He held me close all through the night. If I shifted slightly to switch position in the bed, he pulled me to him. "C'mere," he murmured in his sleep, and pressed his forehead to mine.

It was him: Vittorio who traveled the globe, who filled his days with appointments and rituals to conquer a horror of the void; Vittorio who always had plans, Vittorio the leader; Vittorio, exhausted, who slept with his head on my belly. Vittorio who was afraid of time's passing, of the signs it left on his body. Vittorio, for whom love was a trap that distracted us from ourselves and from the world, against which we had to defend with equal cruelty. Who tried to protect me from my dreams because, for him, giving in to illusion was a weakness for which one paid dearly; that was why he had taken it upon himself to crush each and every one of my expectations, one by one.

Vittorio, who saw meaning only in an awareness of the absurd, and found peace in reading a book as he held me to his chest and stroked my hair with his free hand.

Vittorio who accepted only that which did not require reciprocity. And who had a talent for leaving memories behind, with little effort.

Vittorio, whom I would have loved for better or for worse, forever.

In the morning, as he climbed onto his motorcycle, all I asked him was, "Then we can try?"

"We'll try."

"I'll manage to be with you without smothering you."

"Okay."

"And you?"

"And me?"

"Vittorio!"

"Okay, okay, I won't run away." He laughed.

"All I ask is that you make a little bit of room for me in your life."

"We'll try."

He gave a sharp kick to the pedal, the engine fired.

"You won't tell me to go to hell?" he asked.

"For now, no."

The next day I wrote to him. He did not answer. The day after that I suggested we meet, he fudged. It was a busy week, what with meetings and work-related dinners, he couldn't find time for us. I dug my heels in, he wouldn't budge. I tried not to contact him, he did not contact me. He can't be doing this to me, I thought, he can't be. I found it hard to work, just waiting to go back and glance at the phone, hoping to find a call, a message. I drifted around like a ghost, I did load after load of wash, sitting on the floor and staring at the spinning basket.

"I'm sorry, it's a hectic period," he said on the phone.

"So what else is new? I doubt you're sorry."

"You want to check my appointment book? Sorry if I have my own life and other things besides you. And you know what? You're right,

I'm not sorry, because this is the life I chose for myself and these are the obligations that make me happy. And no, I don't want to cancel them, okay? They are part of who I am. I don't have to account for them, and I don't want to. So, now you understand why I did not want this relationship."

"You didn't want it? You asked for time to think about it, you came back to me, and now you're telling me that you didn't want it? What were you thinking about, then? Why did you come back to me? Tell me, what did you come to my house for?"

"I felt like seeing you."

Rage. Growing rage, rage that devours, consumes, drains you. Impotent rage. Swearing to yourself, "Never again." Wondering how you could have come to accept such degradation. Why, why, why. Wanting to punch and kick. Spit in his face. Stamp on his feet. Lose all self-control. Go on like that, until your last ounce of strength is exhausted. Until you slump to the ground, drained. Until he sees the hole he left in you with his superficiality, his selfishness, his vanity, his vacuousness, his cowardice, his insensitive feelings, his facile excuses, his two-bit pride. His inability to pick and choose. His simulating a solidity that he will never have. His pettiness clothed in grandeur.

Telling yourself over and over again: Vittorio, you are a barren desert. You are nothing but a wasteland. There is not a trace of love in you. Not even God would be able to instill a bit of love in that soulless body of yours. So go on, go ahead and travel the globe, take whomever you want to bed, glorify yourself boasting about your work, be admired for being cultured and brilliant. No matter whom or what I run across in life, it can't be worse than you. All you gave me was your body and the shiny patina of your success; the rest, you decided, was not for me. God damn the day I met you, now and forever. Damn you, until the end of your days. Amen.

I smashed Vittorio's gifts. Seeing the pieces on the floor, Gioia said: "Why the hysterics?"

"I'm entitled to a moment of weakness too, aren't I?"

"The cliché of the silly girl who destroys her man's gifts isn't you."

"But you're wrong. That's what I won't forgive him for. I'll never forgive him for it."

"For what?"

"For making me into a cliché."

36

Day Nine.

The body continues sitting up straight. Look, it doesn't slump. It doesn't give up, doesn't surrender to the looming void.

Speculation. That of falling off the chair, assuming the fetal position with forehead resting on the cold floor, relinquishing the oars of this boat that has continued to go where we had not anticipated, and spending our life forever staring at the spot on the floor where we have laid our forehead. Might as well extinguish the eyes on a spot on the floor, deaden the body, rid it of its frenzy to move, to approach other bodies, to acquire objects. Because the body thinks that this is life, and that by pushing ahead—putting one leg forward, then another, moving the mouth and head to the rhythm of sounds that we call words, on and on for the hours and hours and hours that we call days—it is contributing gallantly to the collective delusion.

Might as well forget you'd had desires, forget the harshness with which they were deceived, chewed up, milked, drained. See to it that all that remains of everything—the light on the sea on August mornings, the slimy trail of a snail that crawled on your hand when you were a little girl—is a body tossed on the ground, which someone will come and pick up out of pity, a body that someone will finally care for without asking for care.

Speculation.

Instead, no one falls off the chair, instead, the pen labors over the page and vomits everything onto the sheet of paper, and the fury of the writing says that the body will not fall. No, the body has decided, it will not fall.

"You'd made a promise to me," I reproached him.

The trams came and went, passing one another. At one time I had found poetry in that Milan of taut wires. Us on the sidewalk, prosaic, beaten.

"You too made me a promise. You said you did not want to change me, that you understood that that's the way I am and that I can't be any other way, you too had promised, and, just look, you didn't even hold out two weeks."

"I couldn't do it," I admitted.

"Me either."

I left. So many times I thought, He can't let me go away like this, he won't. And yet.

We made love one last time. His bed seemed so large.

In the first light of dawn, I looked around his room (the bare walls, the stain on one of them, the chair on which he tossed his clothes) and found a familiarity that, sadly, was rendered too late by the awareness that I would never see it again.

Vittorio woke up and, finding me lying beside him, looked at me with something like astonishment. As if he had expected that at the break of day I'd have vanished, evaporated, dissolved: Poof! Antonia is gone, we can spare ourselves the good-byes.

"Are you crying?"

"No," I lied.

"Sure?"

"Hold me, please."

"You're sure you're not crying?"

"Sure."

He pulled away from the embrace. He drew the sheets over our heads, and, in the bluish half-light that enveloped us, touched my face, tracing my features with both hands, feeling like a blind man. His fingers passed over my cheeks, slowly, over my nose, then up to my eyes, stopping at my cheekbones.

Dear God, I thought, he's recording my face before erasing it.

THE PERFECT ALMOND TREE
MUCH LATER, ON TIPTOE

I knocked at old Amilcare's door.

He opened it as he always did, as if each time awaiting a queen.

His eyes widened. "At last! We've been expecting you for months!" To conceal his excitement, he made me a bow.

"Forgive me, forgive me, everyone. It's been . . . difficult."

He hugged me, I smelled the scent of baby powder.

"I was afraid you'd forgotten about us. Thank you for coming."

I could not find words to reply. I could not tell him, "It's good to be here."

"Come in, come in, take off your jacket."

I looked tenderly at the books he made Silvia read, smelled the aroma of his coffee.

"Silvia, tell me about Silvia, have you given her an ending?"

"No, I'm not . . . I'm not so sure anymore . . ."

Old Amilcare straightened up.

"But you knew from the beginning how it would end, you started writing just to get to that ending!"

"Yes, I had an ending. Antonio returns to San F., cured of his hypochondria, because Silvia cured him. Suffering is healed with suffering and is now no longer frightening. That's the gist of it. Antonio comes back to stay. And establishes a home for children with Down's."

"And then?"

"You have to picture the meeting between Silvia and Antonio the way I'd envisioned it. As if Silvia, all the times we imagined her, might take it upon herself to find that person, all the nights when we could almost hear her heart beating wildly at just the thought, so vivid, of his return. And when she sees Antonio approaching on the white, dusty road and her heart skips a beat, it sums up my dream, and that of my mother and my father, and yours and all the world's . . . because that's what would have happened when Silvia found what she had lost: she would have found it for all of us."

"Go on."

"At San F., Antonio restores a farmhouse, a white farmhouse sprawled amid the singing of crickets, and transforms it into the largest, most successful recreational and cultural center for Down's children in the region. He plants almond trees all around the main house, acres and acres of them. You mustn't picture it as a care center, but as a huge almond grove that at night lights up the surrounding countryside. Antonio calls upon Silvia to teach her poems to the children and young people who will live there, because he wants them too to learn to dance and be joyful under an almond tree. Because the almond tree, which gives life to young people like Silvia, the tree, which that afternoon in the church she'd prayed would disappear from the face of the earth so that no one else might suffer as she had, is a perfect tree. And that's what Antonio named the center: The Perfect Almond Tree. And on each trunk of the vast almond grove the children would nail a wooden plaque testifying to the almond tree's perfection. If I had written those pages, Amilcare, you too would have been able to walk on that sunbaked land, feeling the dried clods underfoot and reading: 'The almond tree is a rustic, hardy plant,' 'The almond tree is not very susceptible to diseases and pests,' and similar tributes on the other trunks. 'It's a plant that adapts to many soil types,' 'It is largely drought resistant,' 'No part of the fruit is wasted.' And finally: 'In the myth of Attis, the almond tree is a symbol of pain from which, however, new life may sprout.'"

"And now, what's missing now?" Amilcare asked me.

"Relief, that's what's missing. I really thought it was pain itself that healed pain, if you see what I mean. But if I open my eyes and look around me, I see all too much suffering that knows no relief: pointless. And there are already too many lies, in books and in the revolving of days, for me to attempt to tell another one."

The old man lowered his eyes and, in his disappointment, I discovered that I was wrong: there is no such thing as resignation affording peace to old age, because hope secretly continues its intense workings in us.

"Is that what they taught you during these past months?"

I swallowed.

"And the almond tree," he insisted, "isn't the almond tree the most perfect?"

I bit my lips and remained silent.

"Now you don't see it, but your ending is there. One day, maybe, you'll write it?"

"I don't want to write fairy tales . . . the truth . . ."

"Fairy tales, Antonia? I might be a senile old fool, but I know that we cannot stop believing in life, in its possibilities, which are endless, in the obligation to remain human. And in love, which is something greater than us and always prevails; in the end that's what remains, trust me, it's stronger than everything. It's when we stop believing in these things that it's really over. I think that someday you will write that ending. But now give me that jacket and come into the living room, we'll be warmer there."

He seemed to have cheered up, he smiled and took the jacket from me. "Would you like to read a poem together?"

"Oh no, Amilcare, no poetry." I reached for his hand mottled with spots. "Remember? Poetry is explosive. I prefer tea, for today."

"Tea it is," he said, putting his hand on mine.

37

Yet even in the worst moments, when I'm traveling through the countryside on a train and the image of Vittorio waiting for me on a platform is a boulder crushing my chest, I can't help but think that the world is undeniably beautiful. The colors chasing after one another, the changing landscapes, a white moon pinned to the sky before it darkens. And I can't explain it, but this beauty tempers the pain and at the same time renders me inconsolable. I'm left behind the glass pane. The beauty flies by. Vittorio will no longer be waiting for me at any station.

I think we will meet again someday, Vittorio and I. And then we can pretend to be grown up, worldly, cordially distant. We'll chat at a table in a bar and avoid any delicate subjects, but inevitably we'll step into something. We'll get out of it, him coolly, me floundering. He will notice it, pretend to look around for the waiter to give me time to regain my composure, when he turns back to me I will have repaired a smile. He'll phone a friend to join him, I'll run a hand through my hair. We'll say good-bye with a kiss on each cheek, murmuring, "See you soon." And we will never see each other again.

From the window of yet another train: Spring is shouting out, blossoming almond trees, white cemeteries, freeze-frames of farmers bent over the fields. A half-built farmhouse. Then trees still bare and slender, where are they reaching to, so willowy?

Every now and then memories leap up, I banish them, welcome them back, if I close my eyes, I'm lost. When it hurts too much, I distract myself. But the window calls—all this life, this languor in all its beauty, I don't want it, I don't want it anymore.

This springtime that prods, whispers, that urges. I don't want promises. What is that yellow in the fields, that yellow that explodes? Shhh, hush, hush, it's no use looking for that part of me, if it's still there, it's tired of being seduced.

Do I want to enter every house again, once again imagine myself on that terrace? In this spring light, even the name of a hamlet, white on a blue sign, "San Lorenzo," looks beautiful.

What is it calling to?

No, settle back, the time for enticements is over.

The battle is over.

I am left defeated and at the same time, in some way, safe. The kind of safety with no victory that applies to one who has been there, there where you crumble; where a mere presence throws open doors, fills the sails with wind, turns up the day's sounds in a crescendo. Where you wait—for things to change, for him to return, for hope to release its stubborn grip, for the pain to settle, finally, into resignation. Where you think you can stand firm on your own two legs and be true to yourself, and instead, when you see a man approaching, you think it's him, even if you know it can't be, for a moment you think it's him—and at moments like those, you feel like you've stumbled, your heart dropping like a fruit in your chest.

I have been there, where "no matter what" prevails, and in that phrase, inevitably, every speck of us vanishes. Where you go wholly or you don't go at all.

That, Vittorio will not have. I thought, His name has betrayed him.

But I was wrong: Vittorio is made to be happy, for that charming cheerfulness of his, for his broad smile. For reading a book, swinging in a hammock, for the simple pleasure of a cigarette he's waited for all day.

May life always give you these things, Vittorio Solmani.

These days I say dusk, I don't say sundown. Sunset is too red. For me, not the showy spectacle that takes your breath away, that stirs the emotions, but a restrained twilight that cloaks the contours, that lends magic to the beams of the first headlights the cars turn on, that settles in with no commotion or streaks of color. And within minutes, on treetops, on electrical poles, on the flanks of hills, on roads that climb in and out of tunnels, on phantom railway overpasses, it is already night.

EPILOGUE

Day Ten, the last day: Take three cupfuls from the mixture to be given to three people.

I dip the first cup into the bowl, fill it. The batter drips, spills onto the counter. Anyway, in the end, who will want these three cups?

> *Add to the remaining mixture two cups of flour, one cup of sugar, a cup of olive oil, a half cup of milk. Crumble a half cup of walnuts, dice an apple, add to mixture.*

The food processor's blades do their work efficiently, and by now all that my hands want is to keep busy and get this done.

> *Combine two eggs, two teaspoons of vanilla extract, a packet of yeast, a pinch of salt. Mix.*

Now it really looks horrible. It's a lumpy, yellowish, slightly frothy mass. Are our wishes that scary?

Pour the batter into a cake pan. Bake at 350°F for 40 minutes.
When ready, make your wish.

There, we're done. The kitchen is a battlefield, but I feel a sort of pride in that mess, a kind of excitement.

Though I'm not sure whether I really want to put this heap in the oven. Tomorrow I'll walk into the kitchen, and the bowl with the little amorphous monster will no longer be there.

The oven light goes off, it's reached the right temperature. I put the pan on the lower rack.

I sit on the floor and peer through the glass door.

And suddenly there she is, Silvia, on all fours next to me.

"It doesn't look so bad, after all," she says, looking up from the oven window. "Can I make a wish too?"

But the next moment she's already gone.

So now I'm alone. We are alone.

You're growing bigger. I, however, have the feeling I've gotten smaller. I'm tired, exhausted. But you're rising. A little too much on one side, in a shapeless, capricious way, but you're rising. You don't mind the heat. The air bubbles you're composed of stretch and swell, your mass grows, your surface acquires color.

I get on my knees to see better, my face so close to the oven, it feels boiling hot. Look at that, Antonia, a horrendous mixture that becomes a cake. So then, magic charms really still exist?

I close my eyes. I make a wish.

ABOUT THE AUTHOR

Claudia Serrano has been working as a bookseller in various Italian cities for the past five years. Born in 1984 in the port city of Bari on the Adriatic Sea, she has always had a way with words. A well-respected freelance journalist, Claudia has won many awards, including the Premio di giornalismo Franco Sorrentino for an investigation into the world of the seeing impaired in Bari. She also holds a bachelor of arts degree in modern philology. *Never Again So Close* is her first novel.

ABOUT THE TRANSLATOR

Anne Milano Appel, PhD, was awarded the Italian Prose in Translation Award (2015), the John Florio Prize for Italian Translation (2013), and the Northern California Book Award for Translation–Fiction (2014, 2013). She has translated works by Claudio Magris, Primo Levi, Giovanni Arpino, Paolo Giordano, Roberto Saviano, Giuseppe Catozzella, and numerous others. Translating professionally since 1996, she is a former library director and language teacher, with a BA in Art and English Literature (UCLA), an MLS in Library Services (Rutgers), and an MA and PhD in Romance Languages (Rutgers).